FROM THE
NANCY DREW FILES

THE CASE: Nancy investigates a case of corporate espionage in the high-stakes world of high fashion.

CONTACT: Beau Winston has discovered you can't make a name for yourself in fashion without making enemies along the way.

SUSPECTS: Mimi Piazza—Beau Winston's number one rival, she'd welcome the opportunity to stab her competition in the back.

Michael Rockwell—The billionaire is openly opposed to his daughter's wedding, and the theft of her gown fits in with his plans.

Angel Ortiz—Beau's design assistant, he resents his boss for hindering his career and may now have designs for revenge.

COMPLICATIONS: Nancy believes she's on the verge of sewing up the case when her top suspect turns out to be a victim . . . of murder!

Books in The Nancy Drew Files® Series

Available from ARCHWAY Paperbacks

The Nancy Drew Files

Case 89
Designs in Crime
Carolyn Keene

AN ARCHWAY PAPERBACK
Published by POCKET BOOKS
New York   London   Toronto   Sydney   Tokyo   Singapore

AN ARCHWAY PAPERBACK *Original*

An Archway Paperback published by
POCKET BOOKS, a division of Simon & Schuster Inc.
1230 Avenue of the Americas, New York, NY 10020

Copyright © 1993 by Simon & Schuster Inc.
Produced by Mega-Books of New York, Inc.

ISBN: 0-671-79481-7

First Archway Paperback printing November 1993

10 9 8 7 6 5 4 3 2 1

NANCY DREW, AN ARCHWAY PAPERBACK and colophon
are registered trademarks of Simon & Schuster Inc.

THE NANCY DREW FILES is a trademark
of Simon & Schuster Inc.

Cover art by Tricia Zimic

Printed in the U.S.A.

IL 6+

Designs in Crime

Chapter

One

WAIT A SEC, Nancy," Bess Marvin said, stopping at the perfume counter on the first floor of Mitchell's, one of New York City's largest department stores. "This is the new fragrance in all the ads."

"No time for shopping," Nancy Drew said. "We have only five minutes to get to the offices on the eighth floor." She poked her head above those of the milling shoppers and spotted the escalators.

Bess pushed up the sleeve of her leather jacket, picked up a tester, and sprayed the cologne on her wrist. "Mmm," she said, sniffing as she followed Nancy onto the escalator. "It's like flowers—and cinnamon! What do you think?" Bess extended her wrist to Nancy.

1

THE NANCY DREW FILES

"It's nice," Nancy agreed, watching the first floor disappear as the escalator rolled upward. They rose past a display of mannequin legs showing off the latest in hosiery.

"Wow!" Bess exclaimed. "Look at those stockings with the little hearts on the side!"

"They're cute," Nancy said, smiling as she unbuttoned her wool blazer. "But you'll have to restrain yourself from bargain hunting until after we meet with Jill. She's the reason we made this trip, remember."

Jill Johnston was a vice-president of the department store. Nancy had earned the older woman's trust when she solved a mystery that saved Mitchell's Thanksgiving Day Parade. An urgent phone call from Jill the day before had prompted Nancy and Bess to pack their bags and fly to New York City right away.

Nancy's aunt, Eloise Drew, had met the girls at the airport that Monday morning. Eloise made time to take the girls to her apartment and then to lunch before driving upstate to visit friends. She'd given the girls a key to her apartment, in Manhattan's Greenwich Village.

"I wish Jill had told you more about why we're here," Bess said as they passed the toy department on the third floor.

"She didn't want to go into detail over the phone," Nancy explained. "But she made it clear that a friend of hers needs help. Jill did say he's a

2

well-known fashion designer whose creations are being ripped off."

"Fashion espionage! Too bad she didn't mention his name," Bess said. "The suspense is killing me."

"At least you've done your homework," Nancy teased. "You've been reading nothing but fashion magazines since we boarded the plane in Chicago."

"One of us should be on top of what's happening in the fashion world," Bess said. "My clothes sense just might come in handy on this case."

"That's true," Nancy said as she stepped off the escalator on the sixth floor.

Then she and Bess headed for an elevator marked Employees Only. After checking their names against a list, a uniformed guard allowed them to board the elevator. It rose swiftly, and in moments the doors opened on the eighth floor. "Here we are," Nancy said as she and Bess stepped into a reception area.

"I'm Nancy Drew, and this is Bess Marvin," Nancy told the receptionist. "We have a one-thirty appointment with Jill Johnston."

The woman behind the desk picked up the phone and notified Jill. Nancy was just about to sit down when a tall woman in her forties with wavy chestnut hair came hurrying down the hall.

"Bess! Nancy!" Jill rushed forward to greet the girls. "You are a sight for sore eyes. And what a hectic week! I just found out that I have to fly to Tokyo on business tomorrow. It couldn't have come at a worse time. But I'm glad you could make it here on such short notice."

"You didn't go into detail on the phone," Nancy said, pushing her reddish blond hair behind her ear. "But you said it was important."

"It is," Jill stated worriedly. "Beau and I have been friends for years, and I'd hate to see his business ruined."

"Beau?" Bess said, her blue eyes flashing. "Do you mean Beau *Winston?*"

Jill nodded. "He's meeting us downstairs, in the bridal salon," she explained. "I thought it would be easier for Beau to explain the problem to you than for me to do it secondhand."

"Sounds good," Nancy said. A moment later she and Bess were following Jill out of the reception area and down the corridor.

When they reached a bank of freight elevators, Jill pressed the down button, then turned to Bess. "Beau will be tickled that you've heard of him. Fame is still fairly new for him."

"I've *always* loved the gowns he designs for Beau Bridal," Bess said.

Turning to Nancy, Jill explained, "Beau's specialty is bridal attire and dressy gowns. He owns and operates his own studio, and his collection, Beau Bridal, has been quite successful."

"And his business can only get better," Bess

4

added. "His name has been in nearly every fashion magazine article since he was chosen to design the Rockwell wedding gown."

"Joanna Rockwell?" Nancy said. "The heiress who's marrying that race-car driver?"

"Exactly," Jill said. "When Joanna got engaged, she looked at bridal fashions from dozens of designers."

"But in the end, she chose Beau's design," Bess said. "What a dream romance! Twenty-two-year-old heiress to wed a hunk race-car driver."

As the elevator whirred down to the sixth floor, Nancy tried to remember everything she'd read about what reporters were calling "the wedding of the century." She knew that Joanna's father, Michael Rockwell, was a billionaire, and the wedding of a billionaire's daughter was always news.

"When is the wedding?" Nancy asked.

"This Saturday," Jill and Bess answered together, then smiled at each other.

"It's getting tons of publicity—like a royal wedding," Bess said. "One photographer even ran through Central Park alongside their hansom carriage just to get a picture of them kissing!" she added.

"Through it all Joanna has been a good sport," Jill said. "Her bright smile and unflappable sense of humor have made her the darling of the press. I think the theft of Beau's designs has to be

5

related to his newfound fame. His association with Joanna has brought him into the limelight more than ever.

"Sixth floor, bridal salon," she announced, holding the elevator doors open for the girls.

Nancy was still thinking about what Jill had said as they arrived in the bridal salon. Although the rest of the store had been crowded with shoppers, the bridal salon was empty and quiet. Framed by a scallop-shell-shaped archway, it was decorated in creamy shades of white with satin fabric on the walls and a trim of lace and velvet bows.

"I'm in heaven," Bess said, circling a mannequin dressed in an exquisite ivory gown before checking out a display of white hats and veils.

From the corner of her eye, Nancy saw a salesperson approaching. The tall, dark-skinned woman with high cheekbones wore a simple maroon knit dress. She paused in front of the girls, then blinked when she recognized Jill.

"Ms. Johnston," she said, smiling. "Is there something I can help you with?"

"Not at the moment, Nola," Jill answered. "We're meeting Beau Winston here to go over some of his designs carried by Mitchell's."

"No problem," Nola said, picking up a headpiece from the display in front of Bess. "Would you like to try it?" she asked, lifting the braided satin headband and spray of lace over Bess's head.

"I'd love to," Bess said, blushing. "But I'm not getting married—at least not at the moment."

"It never hurts to dream," the woman said. Gently she placed the headband over Bess's blond hair and arranged the veil over her face.

"What do you think?" Bess asked, posing for Nancy and Jill.

"Beautiful," Nancy said.

"Try one of the hats," Jill suggested.

Bess tried on a wide-brimmed picture hat.

"You look like a southern belle," Nancy said, handing Bess a veil with a sequined headband.

As Bess tried on one headpiece after another, Nancy wondered if her best friend was thinking of Kyle Donovan, the new guy in Bess's life. Nancy had to admit that here, surrounded by bridal gowns, her own thoughts had strayed to Ned. Tall, smart, adorable Ned Nickerson was definitely the guy of Nancy's dreams, even though she wasn't ready to be a bride yet.

The saleswoman was helping Bess adjust a crown made from satin lilies of the valley when Nancy saw a man in his late twenties come in through the arched salon entrance. He had a bulky garment bag draped over one shoulder. Dressed in black jeans and a bomber jacket, he was a tall, lean silhouette in stark contrast to the white salon. Nancy watched as his dark eyes scanned the room before locking on Jill.

At that moment Jill spotted the man, too. "Hi, Beau!" she called, waving him over.

"Jilly!" He crossed the room and gave Jill a hug, while Bess fumbled to remove the headpiece and smooth her hair. "Sorry I'm late, but I was halfway here when I remembered I needed this," he said, holding up the garment bag.

"Beau, this is Nancy Drew," Jill said, introducing the girls, "and Bess Marvin."

"Thanks for coming," Beau said. As he shook hands with her, Nancy studied Beau Winston. He had dark, serious eyes and brown hair pulled back in a ponytail. Nancy liked the way he looked her right in the eye.

"It's a pleasure to meet you, Mr. Winston," Bess said. "I just love your designs."

"Please, call me Beau," he said, hanging the garment bag on a nearby rack. "I'm flattered that you know my work."

"When it comes to fashion, Bess is right on top of things," said Jill.

Bess shrugged. "It's a hobby of mine."

"That's great! It will help you understand my problem," Beau said, unzipping the garment bag.

Jill touched the saleswoman on the arm and asked, "Nola, would you please bring us the blue beaded Budget Fashions dress from the back?"

With a nod, Nola disappeared into a doorway marked Private near the dressing room. Beau reached into the garment bag and pulled out a shimmering gown in a deep shade of blue. "This is one of my new dresses," he said, lifting the full chiffon skirt so that it billowed gracefully.

"It's gorgeous!" Bess said, running her fingers over the white and silver beaded design on the fitted bodice.

"I just designed it," Beau said. "This is a sample, which I intended to introduce in my spring show next week."

Just then the saleswoman returned, carrying a pale blue dress. "Here's the gown you asked for, part of the new line from Budget Fashions," she said as she hung the gown beside Beau's sample.

"Budget Fashions is a discount manufacturer that makes dresses cheaply and sells them to consumers at a fraction of the cost of designer labels," Jill explained.

"This is one of the dresses Budget is already manufacturing," Beau said, lifting the skirt of the pale blue dress so that the girls could get a better look.

"It's a copy of yours!" Bess exclaimed. "But not nearly so nice."

Touching the skirt of the Budget dress, Nancy frowned. Although it mimicked Beau's design, the fabric felt cheap and the stitching was uneven. "This feels as if it's made of polyester, and the color looks washed out," she said.

"My dress is made of chiffon and silk," Beau said, "and it comes in deep shades—cobalt blue and scarlet." He turned away from the two dresses, as if the sight of the cheap imitation hurt him.

"Your design would have been copied a while

ago," Nancy said. "Who do you think could have stolen it?"

"That's why I wanted to meet you here—away from my studio," Beau said, lowering his voice. "The only way this design could have gotten out of my studio was through someone on my design team."

His black eyes fixed on Nancy as he added, "One of my own people is stabbing me in the back!"

Chapter

Two

So YOU THINK someone on your staff is a spy, working for Budget," Nancy said.

Beau nodded. "Only a handful of people see my completed designs. I hate to accuse any of my employees, but I have to be realistic and I have to stop the thefts. Budget is already manufacturing knockoffs of three designs that I'd planned to show next week."

"Do you have a suspect?" Nancy asked gently.

Beau frowned. "It's got to be someone who knows my designs well. I have two key employees who I share everything with, but I don't think they'd betray me. I—I just don't know. Maybe it's one of my design assistants."

"What a shame," Bess said, admiring the chiffon skirt of Beau's gown. "The imitation doesn't do justice to your design."

"And the cut of the Budget gown is all wrong. My dress really comes to life on a model," Beau added, nodding at Bess. "You look as if you're the right size for this sample. Do you want to try it on?" he asked.

Bess's eyes lit up. "I'd love to—if I can."

"Sure," said Jill. "It will give us a better idea of how Beau's design differs from Budget's."

"Right this way," Nola said, taking the deep blue gown from the rack and leading Bess into the changing rooms.

"You mentioned that you're presenting your spring designs next week," Nancy said. "How often do you have a show?"

"Twice a year," Beau explained. "All the New York designers are showing their spring fashions over the next two weeks. Six months from now, in April, we'll bring out our fall fashions."

"Can you sue Budget Fashions for stealing your designs and selling the knockoffs?" Nancy asked.

Beau frowned. "The chances of winning a case like that are slim," he told Nancy. "Not to mention the sky-high legal fees—which I can't afford."

"Knockoffs are so common in the fashion industry that everyone has come to accept them," Jill explained. "At every fashion show in town, you'll see people in the audience sketching as the models walk down the runway. Within days, they'll be using those designs to manufacture low-priced garments. It's not unusual for a design to be copied *after* a show. But when it happens before a show, it's fashion espionage."

"Do you think you can help me, Nancy?" Beau asked earnestly. "I've got to catch the spy in my studio before whoever it is sells off all my ideas."

"I'll give it my best shot," Nancy said.

Just then Bess emerged from the dressing room. The cobalt blue of the dress complemented the pink glow of Bess's skin. The shiny silver and white beads accentuated her shimmering blond hair, and the tight bodice gracefully hugged her curves.

"You look fabulous!" Jill exclaimed.

"That's definitely your color," said Nancy.

"What do *you* think?" Bess asked, twirling around once before beaming at Beau.

"This dress was made for you," Beau agreed, stepping forward to kneel in front of Bess. "Except for the hemline." He folded the hem up a few times until it reached the bottom of Bess's knees. "That's more like it."

"I know I'm not tall enough to be a model," Bess admitted. "But it's great fun trying on a gorgeous creation like this."

"We do tend to design with tall women in mind," Beau said, rocking back on his heels to peer up at Bess. "But you'd be perfect for a new label I've been planning—a line called Petite Elite."

"I'm five four," Bess said, "so I guess I'd qualify for that line."

"Would you be interested in modeling for me in my studio?" Beau asked. "There are a few dresses in my new collection that might suit someone of your proportions—shapely but shorter than our regular models."

"Your Petite Elite line sounds like a label Mitchell's would be interested in," Jill said thoughtfully.

Bess was astounded. "You want *me* to be a model?"

"I wouldn't expect you to do any photographic or runway work. Just in the studio. Studio models are hired for their perfect proportions."

"It might be a good way for you to help me find the spy at Beau's studio," Nancy added.

"I can't believe this is happening!" Bess said, throwing up her arms. "Of course I'll do it. It's a dream come true!"

"Great!" Beau said, and Nancy was happy to see a smile soften the hard lines of his face for a moment. "If you want to start now, we can share a cab back to my studio. I've got a three o'clock fitting with Joanna Rockwell."

"Joanna Rockwell!" Bess said, scurrying toward the dressing room. "This is going to be so much fun."

As soon as Bess had changed, Jill walked them to the elevator.

"I guess it's time for me to say goodbye," Jill said reluctantly.

Beau gave her a hug. "Have a good trip to Japan."

"My return flight is booked for Sunday," Jill told Nancy. "I'll call as soon as I get back to check on your progress."

"If I know Nancy, she'll have the whole case solved by then," Bess said with a smile.

"Maybe we should get out and walk," Beau suggested as their cab crawled across Fortieth Street.

In front of them a truck had the street jammed as workers unloaded boxes from the back. The cab driver tried to cut around the truck but had to slam on the brakes when a stocky man rolled a rack of plastic-covered dresses right into the street, just inches from the taxi's bumper.

"That was close," Bess said.

"Welcome to the garment district," Beau said, checking his watch. "In this part of town, walking is the best way to get around. My studio is just two blocks away."

He paid the driver, then they climbed out of the cab. On the way to his studio, Beau pointed out a shop that specialized in gloves and a wholesaler that sold buttons by the pound.

Nancy noticed that the buildings were old, with graying cornices and grimy windows. But everyone on the streets hummed along at an energetic clip, moving merchandise and making deliveries.

"This is it," Beau said, turning toward a tall brick building with double glass doors for an entrance. He pulled a metal key ring from his pocket and selected a gold key. "My studio takes up the entire fourth floor. The rest of the building is occupied by suppliers."

Watching Beau unlock the door, Nancy wondered about the security system in the building, but there was no time to ask about it right then. Joanna Rockwell was to arrive in five minutes.

When the doors of the small elevator opened on the fourth floor hall, Nancy found herself blinking in intense white light.

"What's going on?" Bess asked.

"Cut the lights—it's not her!" someone called.

The bright light faded, and Nancy walked from the elevator car into a cluster of people with cameras and microphones.

"Sorry about that," said a slender woman with shoulder-length silver hair. Wearing a red silk suit and a fair amount of makeup, the woman was elegant. Nancy thought she recognized her as a TV news reporter. "We're waiting for Joanna Rockwell," the woman explained.

"Delia," Beau grumbled, "I can't have you bugging my clients."

"Give me a break, Beau," she snapped. "You're her designer, not her publicist."

16

Beau folded his arms and gave the woman's crew a stern look. "Out of the building—now."

The woman started to scowl but forced a smile instead. "Oh, come on, Beau. It's just a fluff piece for 'Fashion Flash.'"

Bess leaned close to Nancy to whisper, "That's the national news segment that highlights fashion events. Delia Rogers is the fashion reporter."

"Think of all the potential clients who might come calling after they see your face on TV," Delia said to Beau.

From the dark expression in his eyes, Nancy could see that Beau would not back down. "Right now I'm more concerned about protecting the privacy of—"

Just then the elevator bell dinged, and everything happened at once.

"There she is!" a man on the camera crew shouted.

Nancy watched as the elevator doors slid open to reveal a petite young woman standing alone in the car. Bright lights flooded the area again as the crew surged forward. Startled, the young woman held her hands over her face.

"Ms. Rockwell, are you happy with the progress Beau has made on your gown?" Delia asked, shoving her microphone toward the young heiress.

So this is Joanna Rockwell, Nancy thought, taking in the pretty brunette who lowered her hands and blinked several times as her eyes adjusted to the bright light. Then, almost without missing a beat, she smiled and said, "Beau Winston's gown makes me feel like a princess."

Before Joanna could take another step forward, Delia fired off more questions. "Any prewedding jitters? Has your fiancé seen the gown? Where are you going for your honeymoon?"

"So many questions! I don't know where to begin," Joanna said lightly. "But if I don't get moving, I'll be late for my last fitting, and Mr. Winston will never forgive me." She glanced over at Beau and winked. "Isn't that right, Mr. Winston?"

"Absolutely," Beau said, taking Joanna by the arm and escorting her past the camera crew to the door of his studio. Nancy and Bess pushed past them, too, and managed to squeeze in behind Beau and Joanna just before the door was firmly shut by a small woman with black hair shot through with gray strands.

"Good riddance!" she said, locking the door. "I told them to go away, Mr. Beau, but do they listen?" She waved at the door disgustedly, then moved toward Joanna. "I'll take your coat, miss. We're ready for you in the fitting room."

"And hello to you, Mrs. Chong," Joanna teased, slipping out of her leather jacket and handing it to the small woman, who scurried out of the reception area.

"That was Mrs. Chong, my sample maker and

right hand," Beau explained to Nancy and Bess. "And this is Joanna Rockwell, who, as you can see, travels with an entourage of reporters."

"I'm Nancy Drew, and this is Bess Marvin," Nancy said, shaking Joanna's hand.

"I've been reading all about you," Bess told Joanna.

"Gee," Joanna said, wincing, "I hope you've read nothing but the good stuff. Some writers really roast me."

"Nancy's a detective who's—" Beau hesitated to glance at Nancy. "She's here to evaluate my security system," Beau said. "And Bess is modeling for me now."

"You handled that woman and her camera crew with finesse," Nancy told Joanna. "I'm sure it's not easy."

"I'm used to the prying eye of the camera," Joanna said, shrugging. "Though I'm determined not to let the media see my wedding gown until I walk down the aisle on Saturday. I think there are some traditions a girl should uphold."

Nancy liked Joanna's attitude.

"Your gown is in the vault," Beau told Joanna. "Right this way."

He led her through a large, sunny workroom just off the reception area, where a handful of people were measuring and cutting fabric on huge tables. Nancy noticed Mrs. Chong tucking and pinning a pink gown on a dress form, while beside her a young man sketched on a tablet.

Walking briskly, Beau took them through a doorway to the left and down a narrow hall.

"Do you really keep the gown locked in a safe?" Bess asked.

"The vault is a secure room where we store the new samples," Beau explained as he paused in front of a steel door at the end of the hall. He unlocked the door with a magnetic card key and flicked on the light.

Curious about the setup of the vault, Nancy entered right behind him. Three walls of the room were lined with racks holding gowns, which were covered with clear plastic. In the center of the room sat an ornate gold rack.

"Wait a minute," Beau said, pausing in front of the empty gold rack. "It should be right here. Where is it?" He crossed to one wall of the room, frantically pushing gowns aside on the rack.

"Maybe Mrs. Chong took it to the fitting room already," Nancy suggested.

"She'd never leave it there unattended." Beau ran to the doorway and shouted, "Mrs. Chong!"

"You mean, the gown is missing?" Bess asked.

Noticing the stricken look on her friend's face, Nancy said, "Let's not jump to conclusions. I'm sure it's here somewhere." Nancy could hear Beau out in the hall, barking questions and orders at his staff. Their voices rose as the word spread.

Mrs. Chong appeared in the doorway, her jaw dropping open when she spotted the empty rack.

She lapsed into Chinese for a moment, then threw up her hands.

"Where is it?" Beau asked her.

"I don't know! I don't know where it could be," Mrs. Chong cried. "Someone must have stolen Joanna's gown!"

Chapter
Three

"STOLEN?" Joanna gasped as the color drained from her face. "That—that's impossible." Turning to Beau, she added, "Isn't it?"

"Well—yes," Beau said, bewildered.

Joanna buried her face in her hands for a moment, then quickly raised her head as if struck by a new thought. "What about the bridesmaids' gowns?" she asked.

Beau hurried over to a row of emerald green dresses and counted. "They're all here."

Nancy realized Joanna was near tears. She touched her arm and suggested, "Why don't you sit down while Beau's staff searches for your dress?"

"But I'm willing to help," Joanna began, her voice cracking with emotion.

"Let us take care of it," Beau said. "You wait in

the fitting room with Bess. Mrs. Chong will show you the way."

As Mrs. Chong led Bess and Joanna out of the vault, Nancy's mind was racing. If the gown had been stolen, it seemed logical that the thief was the same person who had stolen Beau's designs.

"This is my worst nightmare," Beau said, checking through all the dresses in the vault a second time. "Nothing has ever been stolen from the vault."

"There's still a chance that the dress was misplaced, isn't there?" Nancy asked him.

Beau bit his bottom lip. "A slim chance. The staff is turning the place upside down right now. My design assistant, Angel, will report to me when they're done."

Nancy had already paced most of the perimeter of the windowless room, checking for even the slightest cracks in the walls and ceiling. "How could a thief break into this room without leaving a trace?" she asked, thinking out loud. But the bare walls held no answers. She turned to Beau, who was shifting two gowns on the racks. "Make sure there are no cracks or holes in the wall behind those dresses. I didn't look there."

"Will do," Beau said, shoving a sheer black gown to one side so he could check.

Kneeling beside the only door to the vault, Nancy examined the lock. "There are no scratch marks," she told Beau, "no sign that anyone tried to pick the lock—though that would have been a challenge. The magnetic card system used to open this type of lock is hard to derail."

"That's why I had it installed," Beau said, pushing aside an ivory satin bridal gown. "The magnetic strips on the cards are generated by computer, and they have a lot of information encoded on them."

"Besides you, who has a card key to the vault?" Nancy asked.

"Only Mrs. Chong and Angel."

Next, Nancy checked the edges of the gray wall-to-wall carpeting inside the vault. She prodded and tugged, but the carpet was solidly tacked in place. It didn't seem as if anyone could have come through the floor.

"Bad news, boss."

Nancy looked up at the thin man standing in the doorway of the vault. He had thick black hair that fell forward over his forehead and widely spaced brown eyes.

Beau sighed and turned away from the rack of dresses. "You didn't find it?"

"Sorry," the young man said, shrugging.

Quickly Beau introduced Nancy to his assistant, Angel Ortiz. He pointed down the hall. "Tell the staff we're meeting in the workroom— *now*. I want to get to the bottom of this."

The mood was somber as Nancy and Beau entered the large, sunny workroom. Angel boosted himself up to sit cross-legged on top of a table. Mrs. Chong was standing beside a window, no expression on her face. A handful of workers sat on tables and scattered chairs.

"As you all know," Beau began, "the Rockwell gown is missing. I put it in the vault last night when I finished working on it. Has anyone seen it since?"

The unanimous answer was no. "Most of us don't go near the vault," said a tall, exotic-looking model, whom Beau called Isis.

"Has anyone heard or seen anything out of the ordinary today—or last night?" Nancy asked.

Again, people shook their heads.

One girl, wearing a black sweater and tights, flung a golden braid of hair off her shoulder and sighed.

"What's the problem, Eleni?" Beau asked.

"It's not fair to suspect us," Eleni told him. "Most of us were out of here by six yesterday."

"Really?" Nancy said.

"Yeah," Eleni went on. "When I left only Beau, Angel, and Mrs. Chong were still here."

Nancy and Beau asked the group a few more questions, but the answers didn't tell Nancy anything.

After Beau sent the staff back to work, he and Nancy returned for one last look in the vault. Mrs. Chong and Angel joined them.

"Now I remember," Mrs. Chong said as she unlocked the door with the card key hung around her neck. "I heard a funny noise last night, while I was in my sewing room."

"What kind of noise?" Beau asked.

"Like something falling to the floor in the workroom," Mrs. Chong said. "I went in to check it but didn't see anything. Maybe a bolt of cloth dropped, maybe not."

Nancy stared at the older woman. "What time was it?"

"Late—sometime at night," Mrs. Chong said brusquely.

Nancy frowned. She wasn't quite sure what to make of Mrs. Chong.

"Where was I when it happened?" Angel asked.

"Gone," Mrs. Chong said, acting almost irritated.

Angel turned to Nancy. "I was here till midnight, so it was after that."

"So you were the last person here last night?" Nancy asked Mrs. Chong.

The woman nodded, her neat bun gleaming under the fluorescent strip lights. "I locked everything up," she said, gesturing with the pair of shears she had inadvertently carried with her to the vault. The handles of the scissors were made of gold-colored metal and elaborately decorated.

"Did you see Joanna's gown in here before you left?" Nancy prodded.

"I didn't notice," Mrs. Chong replied.

Was she hiding something? Nancy couldn't tell. Mrs. Chong could have taken the gown herself, then made up the story about hearing the noise. If the noise *had been* caused by an intruder, there was no sign of a break-in. One thing was clear to Nancy. Since Mrs. Chong and Angel were the only two people—besides Beau—with keys to the vault, she'd have to watch them closely.

"Can you think of anyone who'd want to steal Joanna's wedding gown?" Nancy asked.

Beau rolled his eyes, while Angel and Mrs. Chong exchanged a look.

"That's easy," Mrs. Chong said. "Mimi Piazza would love to see Mr. Beau fall flat on his face."

"She's been a rival of mine since we went to design school together," Beau admitted. "Mimi specializes in bridal and evening wear, too."

"And her design was second choice for Joanna Rockwell's gown," Angel added.

"When Joanna chose Mr. Beau's design, Mimi blew up," Mrs. Chong explained. "Steaming like a kettle! Now she really hates us."

"I'll see what I can find out about Mimi Piazza," Nancy said to Beau. "But right now we'd better tell Joanna what's going on."

"Exactly what I've been dreading," Beau said, wearily rubbing his eyes. "That girl's going to be heartbroken, and it's all my fault." He headed for the fitting room with Nancy following.

Joanna's face lit up when they first walked in, but a moment later her smile faded. "No luck?"

"I'm afraid not," Beau said. He sat beside her on the couch and squeezed her arm. "I'm so

27

sorry. I can't imagine how this happened, but I'm going to get to the bottom of it."

"Maybe it'll turn up," Bess said hopefully.

"That gown was very special to me," Joanna said as tears filled her eyes. "Did Beau tell you that he designed the dress around the bodice of my mother's bridal gown. Her own pearls were sewn in at the neckline. And seed pearls from her gown covered the—the—" Overcome with emotion, Joanna covered her face with her hands.

Upset, Bess asked Nancy, "Did you find any clues? Any signs of a break-in?"

"I haven't had a chance to investigate thoroughly yet," Nancy said. "But I will, and there's a good chance that the missing gown is related to the problem Beau has been having here."

Beau turned to Joanna. "You might as well know why Nancy came here in the first place." He explained about his stolen designs.

"I'd appreciate your help, Nancy," Joanna said. "Bess tells me you're an expert detective. I know it's just a dress. But part of it belonged to my mother. She didn't live long enough to see me walk down the aisle. Wearing her pearls was a way of having her close to me." Joanna wiped a tear from her cheek. "You must think I sound silly and sentimental."

"I think it's a beautiful idea," Bess said.

Nancy nodded. "I'll need to know what I'm looking for. Can you describe the gown?"

"What about the photo?" Beau suggested.

"Good idea." Joanna reached into her purse and fished out a photograph. "Here's a picture of me in the gown," she said, handing Nancy the snapshot. "Beau took it at my last fitting. You can keep it for now—but not a peep to the media."

"I'll guard it carefully," Nancy said, studying the photo. The pearls on the antique white bodice gleamed. In the shot, Joanna was smiling as she lifted the satin train of the full skirt. "Can you think of anyone who has a grudge against you?" Nancy asked Joanna. "An old friend or classmate?"

Joanna paused to consider the question. "Not that I know of. I try to be honest with people. Usually it keeps me out of trouble."

"Maybe your fiancé will have some ideas," Nancy suggested.

"Sam?" Joanna asked. "Why don't you and Bess join us for dinner, and you can ask him. We're dining at my father's apartment, so you'll also have a chance to meet Dad and my brother, Tyler. What do you say?"

"Sounds good to me," Bess said.

"We'd love to join you," Nancy agreed.

"Before you go," Beau said, "why don't you choose another gown from my collection. I'll have it altered in case Nancy can't locate your gown by Saturday."

"I guess it'll be good to have a standby," Joanna said, "but I hope I don't have to wear it."

Beau showed the girls one elegant gown after

another, and Bess fell in love with them all. Joanna wasn't quite as enthusiastic. At last she chose a traditional gown with puffed sleeves and a fitted bodice.

"Excellent choice," Beau said.

Joanna forced a smile, though Nancy sensed that her heart wasn't in it. "Ready to go?" Joanna asked, slipping her jacket on. "My driver is waiting downstairs."

"We'll see you tomorrow," Nancy told Beau as they walked to the studio door.

"I'll be here," Beau said, holding the door open. "I'm really sorry about the gown, Joanna. But we've got a great detective on the case." The girls said goodbye, then crossed to the elevators.

"My head is still spinning," Joanna said, touching her forehead. "I can't believe my gown has been stolen."

"Nan, you've got to find the dress before the wedding," Bess said. "Isn't there some way to—"

"Stolen?" came a voice from out of nowhere.

Nancy spun around as a figure emerged from a shadowy nook beside the elevator bank.

"This *is* a hot scoop," said the silver-haired reporter. It was Delia Rogers. She'd heard every word!

Chapter

Four

JOANNA GASPED at the sight of the TV journalist. "I—I didn't see you there."

Nancy could see that Joanna was too upset to handle Delia with her usual aplomb. "What are you doing here?" Nancy demanded.

"My crew is outside, taping background footage," Delia explained. "I came up to see if the entrance to Beau's studio would make a better shot—but what I got is a plum. When was your gown stolen?" she pressed Joanna. "Is anything else missing? And who's the detective on the case?"

"I—" Joanna hesitated, then blurted out, "Nancy Drew is the investigator, and, uh—"

"Right now it's better if we don't reveal the details of the case," Nancy said, taking charge. As far as she was concerned, Delia Rogers already knew too much. Spotting a doorway marked Stairway, Nancy saw their chance to escape.

"Who do you think stole it?" Delia probed. "Does this mean the wedding is off?"

"You'll have to save those questions for a later date," Nancy said as she took Joanna by the arm and ushered her toward the staircase. Bess snapped to attention and followed.

The girls ducked through the door. They were descending the first staircase when Delia's voice echoed down with more questions.

"Doesn't she ever give up?" Bess muttered under her breath.

"Chances are, she'll take the elevator and beat us down," Nancy speculated as they hurried. "When we get to the lobby, we might be greeted by her and her crew. Just ignore them and keep walking."

When they reached the ground floor and pushed open the staircase door, the crush began. The lobby glowed with the lights of the camera crew, who had surrounded the door.

"Here's the distraught bride now," Delia said into her microphone. "Is there any hope of recovering the gown?" she asked, shoving the mike at Joanna.

"Sorry, Delia, but we're late for dinner," Joanna answered as she made her way past the reporter. A minute later the three girls stepped into the back of a black limousine and sank into the plush seats. The camera crew was still clamoring outside the limo when the driver pulled away from the curb.

Joanna sighed. "I'm glad that's over."

"So much for keeping a low profile," Nancy said as the limo joined the stream of cars heading uptown. "When does Delia's report usually air?"

"'Fashion Flash' is on every morning," Bess answered, turning to Joanna. "I guess you'll be featured tomorrow."

"My father's going to have a fit," Joanna said, staring out the window. "He hates negative publicity."

Twenty minutes later the limousine pulled up at the canopied entrance of a tall building on Fifth Avenue. No sooner had the limo stopped than the door was opened by a uniformed doorman. "Good evening, Miss Rockwell," he said, extending a white-gloved hand to help the girls out of the car.

Nancy climbed out and looked around her. Though it was now dark, she could still make out the majestic old stone and brick buildings that lined this side of Fifth Avenue, across the street from Central Park.

Inside, a guard escorted them through the paneled lobby lit by brass wall sconces. Bess paused in front of a painting and smiled. "It's like a museum."

"I grew up in this building," Joanna said as another guard ushered them into a private elevator. "Our apartment takes up three full floors, but as a kid I felt the real action was downstairs. I used to drive the poor doormen crazy, playing hide-and-seek and other games in the lobby. Sam's and my new apartment isn't nearly so grand as my dad's, but it's a lot cozier."

Upstairs, the elevator opened on a marble-floored foyer.

"Good evening, Miss Rockwell—ladies," a slight, white-haired man in a black suit greeted them.

"Hello, Max," Joanna said, handing him her jacket. "Will you tell cook there'll be two more for dinner?"

"Of course," the butler said, taking Nancy and Bess's coats. "Mr. Hollingsworth has arrived. You'll find him in the library with your father." He nodded, then hurried off.

"Hello," Joanna called, leading Nancy and Bess down the marble-floored corridor to an arched doorway. Inside were rows and rows of books set on the dark wood shelves lining every wall.

Seated in an upholstered chair beside the marble fireplace was Michael Rockwell, the gray-haired billionaire whose broad, beefy face had appeared on the cover of every major business magazine at least once. An unlit pipe was wedged in his mouth, and a newspaper was open on his lap.

"Hi, Daddy." Joanna crossed the room and kissed her father on the cheek.

A young man jumped up from the sofa opposite Rockwell and joined her. So this is Joanna's fiancé, Nancy thought, looking over the solidly built guy with sandy blond hair and hazel eyes. He was wearing faded blue jeans and a cherry red sweater.

"Joanna," he said, going over to kiss her. He paused suddenly and studied her closely. "What's up. I can tell something's wrong."

"Oh, Sam—I have bad news." Joanna's voice cracked as she hugged her fiancé. She remembered her manners and turned to the girls in the door. "Meet Nancy Drew and Bess Marvin," Joanna said. "This is my father, Michael Rockwell, and my fiancé, Samuel Hollingsworth."

"Please, call me Sam," the young man insisted.

"The press calls you Sam Speed, king of the racing circuit," Bess said as she shook his hand.

Sam beamed. "You're a racing fan?"

Dimples appeared in Bess's cheeks as she smiled. "Not really, but I read a lot of magazines."

"Hello, ladies," Mr. Rockwell said. He rose and shook their hands before returning to his chair. "What's this about bad news?" he asked Joanna.

"Don't tell me," said a voice from behind Nancy. A young man in his twenties ambled in.

THE NANCY DREW FILES

His brown hair curled over his collar, and a single gold earring glimmered in one earlobe. The resemblance to Joanna was unmistakable. This must be her brother, Nancy thought.

"Let me guess," the young man said sarcastically. "The flowers have wilted? The cake is missing a layer? Or is it the caterer? He can't get the ice sculpture you want."

"This is my brother, Tyler, the dramatic one in the family. He's an actor. His first off-Broadway show is opening this week," Joanna said, introducing the girls. "Tyler, I know you're sick of hearing about my wedding plans, but this is serious."

Quickly Joanna told how her gown had been stolen and Delia Rogers had overheard the news. "Nancy has offered to help track down the dress, and I jumped at the idea," she finished.

"Now, don't skip ahead, Joanna," Michael Rockwell said. "We can hire the finest investigators money can buy."

"But Nancy's a fantastic detective," Bess insisted. "She's solved some impossible cases."

"No offense, Ms. Drew, but I'd prefer someone with more experience," Mr. Rockwell said.

Standing her ground with the man who was pointing the stem of his pipe at her, Nancy said, "My age has never kept me from solving a mystery."

"Daddy," Joanna said firmly, "Nancy is working on this case, and that's final."

"A stolen gown! Less than a week before your wedding," Mr. Rockwell barked. "I don't like it."

Tyler crossed his arms. "Kind of puts a damper on your big media event, doesn't it, Dad?"

Nancy noticed the tension between the two men even before Michael Rockwell glared at his son.

"What about the material taken from your mother's gown?" Sam asked. "And all her pearls?"

"They're gone, along with the dress," Joanna said sadly. "And I feel awful about it."

"It's a bad omen," Mr. Rockwell warned. "Perhaps the wedding should be canceled."

"Maybe he's right," Joanna said, her eyes filling with tears. "I'm so upset, I don't know what to do."

"Take it easy, Sis," Tyler said.

Sam took her in his arms. "I'm not going to let a wedding dress stand between us," he said gently. "We're getting married this Saturday— even if we have to wear grass skirts! The only thing I care about is *you.*"

"Oh, Sam." Joanna laughed through her tears.

Nancy was touched by Sam's response, although Michael Rockwell clearly was not.

"It's not too late to call the wedding off," Mr. Rockwell said, pacing now in front of the fireplace. "It's the only thing to do. I'll call the caterer right away and—"

"Dad!" Tyler exploded, slamming his fist on a

table to get his father's attention. "There you go again, bulldozing ahead, not listening to a word anyone else says. Didn't you hear Sam and Joanna? They're going ahead with their wedding."

"Nonsense," Michael Rockwell insisted. "I'm just doing what's best for everyone. Of course, we'll have to contact all the guests, and—"

"No!" Tyler interrupted. "Leave Joanna alone!"

"Tyler—" Joanna said, taking his arm. "Take it easy."

"No!" Tyler said, shaking his sister off. He glared at his father. "You can push the rest of the world around, but not Joanna and me!"

Chapter

Five

MICHAEL ROCKWELL glared silently at his son for a full ten seconds. "Has it ever occurred to you that I might know what's best for this family?" he finally growled.

"No. You only know what *looks* best—to the media," Tyler snapped. "Our feelings are never taken into account."

"If you had a head for business, you'd understand how important appearances are." Mr. Rockwell crossed the library to a paneled door that led to an office. "I have a few calls to make," he said, and shut the door behind him.

"I'm out of here," Tyler muttered. "I have a preview tonight."

"Wait," Joanna said, taking his hand. "Talk to me for just a minute, and please try not to be too upset with Daddy."

"He drives me crazy, Joanna—you know that," Tyler said, stepping backward like an agitated colt. "Three months ago he wasn't going to allow this marriage to happen. He wanted you to marry someone with assets, so there could be a merger instead of a marriage."

"But he seems okay with Sam now—" Joanna began.

"Yeah, when he finally realized he couldn't stop your marriage," Tyler interrupted. "So what does he do then? He decides to turn your wedding into a media event, with you and Sam as chief tightrope walkers. All to keep the Rockwell name in the news. It makes me sick, Joanna," he went on, shaking his head. "And you let him do this to you."

She sighed wearily as if she'd heard it all before. "It's not so bad. In fact, I'm having fun. Really." Nancy could tell that fun was the last thing Joanna was having. The young heiress was under pressure from all sides, and Nancy felt deeply sorry for her.

"I just wish you'd reconsider being in the bridal party," Joanna said weakly. "I don't want to put extra pressure on you, and I know the press has been hounding you. But it just won't feel right without you."

"I can't do it," Tyler said coldly. "I don't have time for wedding games. I'm going to the theater. I have to perform tonight." With that he turned and strode toward the penthouse elevator.

"Wow," Bess whispered to Nancy. "He sure left in a huff."

Joanna stood still, staring after her brother.

"Does Tyler argue with your father often?" Nancy asked quietly.

"The fights have gotten worse in the last few years, ever since Tyler announced he was going to be an actor," Joanna said. "My father doesn't approve."

"It's not easy to win her dad's approval," Sam added with a wry smile. "I speak from experience. The old man *hates* racing."

"That's different," Joanna insisted. "Racing is dangerous. Daddy's concerned that you might get hurt." When Sam raised an eyebrow doubtfully, Joanna smiled. "Okay, okay—*I* worry that you might get hurt."

"Your father's main concern is what the guys at his club think," Sam said. "They don't approve of his daughter marrying a mere race car driver."

Joanna rolled her eyes. "They're just jealous because your life is a zillion times more exciting than theirs," she told Sam.

"That's because I'm marrying you," he said, placing a kiss on Joanna's cheek.

Seeing them together, Nancy was glad Sam and Joanna had decided to go ahead with the wedding, despite the missing gown.

"You two need to give me some help," she told the couple. "Is there anyone you can think of who might want to get back at you by stealing Joanna's gown?"

Sam checked with Joanna, then shrugged. "No one that I can think of. I pride myself on not having any enemies. In my business, you have to be a good sport."

Just then Max announced that dinner was served. Bess and Nancy followed the couple through the richly decorated apartment to the dining room, where savory smells filled the air. Mr. Rockwell joined them.

First the maid brought out a green salad. The main course was sole stuffed with crabmeat. Joanna and Sam entertained the other three with humorous stories of their endless wedding preparations while they ate.

"I bet you'll be relieved when it's all over," Nancy said. "Are you going on a honeymoon?"

Joanna's smile faded and Nancy knew she'd touched on a delicate subject.

"Well . . ." Joanna hesitated. "We might spend a few days in Florida."

"Florida!" Mr. Rockwell huffed. "You mean you're going to hang around at some racetrack while Sam wastes his time with a bunch of grease monkeys!"

Sam tossed his napkin on the table, but before he could object, Joanna said, "Daddy, Sam agreed to drive at Daytona long before our wedding plans were set. We'll go on our honeymoon later."

The subject was dropped when a servant appeared with a tray of fruit and pastries. As they finished dessert, Nancy couldn't help thinking there was much more to the Rockwell family than met the eye.

She still was focused on the Rockwells and their problems when she unlocked the door of her aunt's apartment.

Nancy took in the light blue comforters on the freshly made beds in the guest room and sighed. "It's been a long day," she told Bess.

"Can you believe Joanna's father wanted to cancel the wedding?" Bess said as she hung her clothes in the closet and pulled on a nightgown.

Nancy nodded. "I thought it was strange, too. If he was really determined to stop the wedding, Michael Rockwell could easily have hired someone to steal the gown."

"What about the stolen designs?" Bess asked as she flopped back on her bed. "If they are connected to the dress, why would Mr. Rockwell steal Beau's designs and sell them to Budget Fashions?"

"Good question," Nancy agreed. "First thing tomorrow I'm going to call my father and ask him to check out Michael Rockwell."

Early the next day the girls were in the kitchen making breakfast when Nancy remembered "Fashion Flash." "Let's see what Delia Rogers has to say about the stolen gown," Nancy said as

43

she switched on the small television in the kitchen.

"That's right," Bess said. She stifled a yawn as she poured two glasses of juice.

Nancy turned to the right station to find a critic reviewing a new film. She was buttering her toast when she heard a new voice. "This is Delia Rogers with 'Fashion Flash.'"

"There's Delia," Bess said. The girls climbed onto stools at the kitchen counter to watch the program.

"Today's fashion news is loaded with glamour *and* intrigue," Delia said, cheerfully smiling at the camera. "Our crew was on the scene at designer Beau Winston's studio yesterday when we came upon unhappy heiress Joanna Rockwell and detective Nancy Drew."

As Delia spoke, videotape of Joanna, Nancy, and Bess leaving Beau's studio filled the screen. "Hey," Bess said, perking up. "We're on TV, Nan!"

"Too bad," Nancy groaned. Now there was no way to keep a low profile on the case.

"Joanna's bridal gown has been stolen!" Delia said with relish. "The theft is especially poignant since the gown was made from material from Joanna's mother's wedding dress and trimmed in pearls that belonged to Coral Rockwell, who passed away two years ago. What does this mean for the couple?" Images of Sam and Joanna flashed on the screen. In one clip, Sam was wearing the flame-retardant suit of a race car driver. He held a shiny trophy up high before hugging Joanna.

" 'Fashion Flash' can name two people who might benefit from this crimp in the wedding plans. First there's Mimi Piazza—" A closeup of a beautiful woman in her twenties flashed on the screen. With her creamy skin and short red hair that curled in wisps around her face, Mimi looked more like a cover girl than a designer.

" 'Fashion Flash' viewers will recall that one of Mimi's bridal designs was Joanna Rockwell's second choice," Delia explained. "Mimi went ahead and worked up a sample of that design. The dress—a size six, perfect for the petite Joanna—will make its debut at Mimi's show on Thursday."

Delia smiled like a smug cat, adding, "Unless, of course, Joanna now decides to wear Mimi's dress down the aisle. With Beau Winston's gown missing, it may be a possibility.

"Another person who's in no rush to see Joanna at the altar is her father, billionaire Michael Rockwell," Delia continued as the wide pink face of Mr. Rockwell flashed on the screen. "It's no secret that Rockwell does not see eye to eye with his future son-in-law. Sources close to Rockwell say he would love to see Sam Speed disqualified from the race to the altar with his beloved Joanna."

"What a story," Bess said as Delia Rogers

signed off. "Maybe Joanna's father *is* the one behind the missing gown."

Nancy thought the idea through as she finished her toast. "A man with Michael Rockwell's billions could have paid someone on Beau's staff or a thug to steal the gown from the vault. He could have assumed the theft would upset the wedding plans."

"But what about Beau's stolen designs?" Bess asked. "Why would Rockwell want to ruin Beau's design business?"

"Maybe the stolen designs are just a diversion," Nancy suggested. "Only two people were in Beau's studio the night Joanna's gown disappeared—Angel and Mrs. Chong," Nancy went on. "So it seems that both thefts have to be inside jobs."

Bess rinsed off the breakfast dishes. "I'll keep an eye on both of them while I'm modeling at the studio."

"Thanks," Nancy said. "But first I think we should check out Mimi Piazza. She might think she's got a shot at being Joanna's designer. I don't know how she could have managed to steal from Beau, but I'd like to visit her studio this morning to see what we can find out."

"You can begin your research right here," Bess said. "Mimi is mentioned in a lot of the fashion magazines I was reading on the plane."

"Great!" Nancy said.

As Bess ran to get the magazines, Nancy picked

up the phone to call home. She smiled when she heard the warm voice of her father, Carson Drew. "Is this *the* Nancy Drew, as featured on 'Fashion Flash'?" he teased.

"You saw the report!" Nancy said.

"I was a little surprised to see my daughter rubbing elbows with a celebrity bride," Carson said. "What's going on there?"

Quickly Nancy explained the events of the past day, describing the situation at Beau's studio, as well as the tension between Michael Rockwell and his children. "I need a favor. What do you know about Michael Rockwell?" she asked her father.

"The man is in a league of his own," he answered. "From what I've read, he seems to be honest and well-respected. I've never met him, though I do have a colleague who once handled a real estate deal for him."

Carson Drew agreed to see what he could learn about Michael Rockwell. "I'll call you as soon as I have some answers," he told Nancy. "Though I'll probably be seeing you before then—on TV."

"It's possible," Nancy said, laughing.

By the time Nancy hung up, Bess had skimmed a few magazines and marked articles that featured Mimi and her designs.

While Bess took a shower, Nancy studied every photo and blurb she could find on Mimi Piazza. The thin, fragile-looking woman was always pictured in a well-tailored suit with a handkerchief in her breast pocket. Many of the articles mentioned that Mimi was a security freak, with one of the best guarded studios in the garment district.

Bess and I will need a story to get in the door, Nancy thought as she planned their visit to Mimi's studio. I hope she won't recognize us from the videotape on "Fashion Flash."

An hour later Nancy and Bess climbed out of a cab on Seventh Avenue, in front of the impressive white building that took up half the block and housed Mimi Piazza's studio. In the lobby Nancy checked the directory and saw that Mimi's studio occupied the second and third floors.

Next Nancy glanced at the uniformed guard who sat at a wide counter that blocked the elevators. A burly man with a bulldog face, he was intimidating. He nodded at a young man heading in who flashed an ID card, then turned back to Nancy and Bess.

"What can I do for you, ladies?" the guard asked.

"We're here to see Mimi Piazza," Bess said, her cheeks dimpling as she smiled at the man.

"Do you have an appointment?" he asked.

"We're design students at the Fashion Institute," Bess began. "We met Mimi at a lecture she gave last week."

"She said we could stop in for a tour of her

48

studio when we had a chance," Nancy fibbed, without batting an eyelash.

They told the guard their names, and he called the studio. Nancy crossed her fingers as the guard told their story to the person on the other end of the line, then hung up.

"Sorry, ladies," he said. "Ms. Piazza won't be able to see you today."

"There must be some mistake," Nancy insisted. "She's going to be upset when we tell her we were turned away."

The guard wouldn't budge. "I've got my orders, miss. Have a nice day."

Outside the building Nancy said she refused to give up. "There's got to be another way in," she said, studying the building's facade and walking to the end of the block. The driver of a truck was backing his rig into an open loading dock for the building. Two men directed him from the sidewalk.

"There's the loading dock for this building," Nancy said.

Bess nodded. "But we'll never get in that way past those men."

"That's why you have to distract them," Nancy said. "Give me two minutes, then you're on." Leaving Bess behind, Nancy turned the corner and walked beyond the loading dock so she was waiting behind the truck. A minute later she heard Bess exclaim, "Ouch!"

Peering around the truck, Nancy saw Bess collapse to the sidewalk and grab her ankle. "Can somebody help me, please!" she called.

The two men ran to Bess. Nancy heard the door slam on the cab of the truck as the driver joined them.

Seizing her chance, Nancy darted into the quiet loading dock area. In five lunging steps she was up the ramp and facing a narrow door. It wasn't locked. She slipped inside, finding herself in a dimly lit stairwell—the fire stairs.

Mimi's studio is on the second and third floors, she reminded herself. Her pulse raced at the thrill of being inside. She climbed a few steps.

Then Nancy felt a hand close over her shoulder. Another gripped her upper arm and yanked her back down the stairs.

Chapter

Six

STRUGGLING TO STAY on her feet, Nancy stumbled down to the landing. The quick descent sent her twisting around, and suddenly she was face-to-face with the burly guard from the lobby.

"Not so fast," he growled like a bulldog ready to attack. "Hey—you're the girl from before." He darted a look up the stairs, then added, "Where's your friend?"

"She's waiting outside," Nancy answered.

"Well, if you're lying, she won't get far. Nobody ever does." He released Nancy and put his hands on his hips. "So you're a design student? Let's see your student ID."

"I—I didn't bring it with me," Nancy said, clutching the shoulder bag that hung at her side.

"Yeah, sure." The guard screwed up his face as

he assessed her, then pointed her toward a door. Nancy went through the door first and found that she was back in the lobby. From that angle, she could see the half-dozen monitors concealed behind the guard's station.

"I don't know what you kids think you'll find up there," the guard said, "but you're not going to score any points with Ms. Piazza by sneaking into her studio. Next time you won't get off so easily," he warned as he escorted Nancy to the front door.

When Nancy emerged through the main entrance, Bess was waiting there. She did a double take. "What happened?" she asked.

"I got snagged," Nancy said, explaining how she'd run into the guard. "I didn't realize they had surveillance cameras everywhere."

"That place is guarded like a fortress," Bess said. "What next?"

"We can walk over to Beau's studio," Nancy said, heading down Seventh Avenue. "It's only four blocks from here."

"So I guess Mimi Piazza is a dead end," Bess said, turning her head to watch as a man rolled a rack of plaid jumpers in plastic bags past them.

"Not yet," Nancy said, weaving through a group of men who were loading bolts of fabric into a truck. "I'm more determined than ever to check out Mimi Piazza. I just have to figure out how to get close to her."

* * *

When Nancy and Bess arrived at Beau's studio, they found the designer in his office, reviewing sketches with Angel Ortiz. Eager for an update on the case, Beau sent Angel off and closed the door. "Any new developments?" Beau asked the girls.

Nancy told him about her thwarted attempt to sneak into Mimi's studio.

"Kicked out?" Beau winced. "Sorry, Nancy. I could have told you that would happen if I'd known your plan. Nobody gets past the security guards in Mimi's building."

"But there's got to be some way to find out what's going on at Mimi's studio," she said.

"Her show is on Thursday," Beau said. "Mimi always presents her new line at her studio. She's afraid to let her collection leave the building."

"Then we'll go to her show," Bess suggested.

"The only problem is, you need to get on the guest list," Beau pointed out, "and that's impossible unless you're a buyer, a magazine editor, or a celebrity."

"Could Jill get us in?" Bess asked.

"She's in Tokyo," Nancy reminded her.

Beau shook his head. "If you think security was tight today, it's three times as bad the day of a show. You need to get on that list."

"I'll think of something," Nancy vowed. "In the meantime, I'd like to spend the rest of the day here, checking out your security system, your help, your routine."

"Feel free," Beau offered.

"I think I need to know a little more about your key employees," Nancy said, hedging a little.

"Let me guess," Beau said. "You want to know why I put up with Mrs. Chong's attitude."

Bess rolled her eyes. "The woman's about as subtle as a bulldozer—and she scares me."

Beau smiled. "Ah, but there's a heart of gold inside that bulldozer. Mrs. Chong hasn't had it easy. She fled China years ago and came here with just the clothes on her back and her incredible sewing ability."

"And what about Angel?" Nancy asked.

"His family moved to New York from Puerto Rico when he was a kid," Beau explained. "We met when I gave a speech at a design institute where he was a student. He's bright and talented."

"Does he ever design for you?" Bess asked.

"He's always sketching," Beau said, "but none of his designs have worked for me yet. I know he'll break through one of these days.

"Anything on Joanna's gown?" Beau asked. "I know it's early."

"Not yet," Nancy told him. "We spent the evening with her family and fiancé last night, but I still don't have any clues about her gown."

"What a mess," Beau said. "We're working against the clock, trying to finish designs for next week's show. Meanwhile, Mrs. Chong is tied up, altering the substitute gown that Joanna is less than thrilled with." Frustrated, he raked his fingers through his long hair. "This studio has seen better times."

"For now you need to focus on getting your collection ready for next week," Nancy said. "I'll do my best to find your leak—*and* Joanna's gown."

"In the meantime I'll be putting you to work," Beau said, turning to Bess. "Angel and I have picked out some gowns we'd like to alter for the Petite Elite line. If you try them on, one of my assistants will pin the hems and mark the other alterations."

"Let's go!" Bess said, jumping to her feet.

While Beau and Bess went off to work on Petite Elites, Nancy got to work on the case.

Nancy thought through what she knew, which wasn't much. She did know that Budget Fashions was producing the knockoffs of Beau's designs. She decided that maybe she could find the thief through his or her connection to Budget.

Pulling a phone book down from Beau's bookcase, she found a listing for Budget and called the number. The woman who answered told her the showroom was open only to retail buyers.

Another obstacle, Nancy thought as she hung up the phone. If Jill were in town, she could use Mitchell's clout to get Nancy in, but Jill was in

Tokyo. Somehow Nancy had to find a way to do some investigating at Budget Fashions.

She called Jill's assistant at Mitchell's and explained the problem. The woman said she'd mention it to Jill when she called in. Nancy thanked her, then hung up.

In the meantime she could work the case from this end. Beau was sure that someone on his staff had to be the thief. Still, Nancy had to wonder how hard it would be for someone else—such as Mimi Piazza or Michael Rockwell—to break into the studio.

She started by checking the main entrance on the first floor. Unlike Mimi's building, no guard was stationed in the lobby.

Nancy pulled open one of the glass doors at the main entrance and inspected the lock. "A cinch!" she said, testing the way the bolt fit against the striker plate. A burglar could slip a thin piece of plastic—like a credit card—between the two parts of the lock. The door would open in seconds.

Nancy was about to close the door when the elevator opened and Eleni, one of Beau's employees, emerged carrying two plastic sacks.

"Guess who scored today's errands—and trash detail?" Eleni said wryly.

Nancy held the door open, then peeked outside to watch the girl walk to a metal Dumpster in front of the building and toss both bags in.

Another security risk, Nancy thought. Anyone

walking by could pick through the trash to find discarded sketches of Beau's designs.

Maybe the lock on the studio door is stronger and more efficient, she thought. But when she reached the fourth floor, she found that the door to the studio was unlocked. A sophisticated lock and alarm panel was built into the wall beside the studio door, but it wasn't activated.

The staff probably turned on the alarm only when they locked up at night. During the day anyone could sneak items out.

Inside the studio, Nancy went into the workroom and found Bess wearing an ice pink satin gown. Kneeling at her feet, a young woman was pinning up the hem.

"Isn't this gorgeous?" Bess asked, smoothing the material over her waist and touching the tiny satin-covered buttons that ran up the front. "They're going to take up the hem and shorten the bodice for women with my proportions."

"It's lovely," Nancy agreed, dodging an assistant who was carrying a bolt of fabric over his shoulder. The room buzzed with activity. Supervised by Angel, Mrs. Chong, and Beau himself, workers moved through their tasks, their fingers deftly stitching, pinning, or cutting.

Sunlight streamed in through the tall, arched windows along the outer wall. An adjacent wall contained floor-to-ceiling shelves full of binders and black portfolios. Against a third wall, bolts of material were stacked haphazardly. The center of the room was dominated by two large work-tables.

Mrs. Chong tugged a bolt of lace from the stack, tucked it under her arm, then turned to Nancy. "You better find that gown—*soon,*" she barked at Nancy. "I'm sewing like crazy, and still I know Miss Rockwell won't be happy." She snorted, then charged off to her sewing room, little more than a cubicle in the corner, attached to the workroom by a narrow door.

"Don't let her bother you," Angel said, smiling up from his sketch. "Mrs. Chong is abrupt, but she means well." He was drawing a gown that was on a dress form, a padded replica of a woman's torso that stood on a metal stand, like a statue without arms, legs, or a head.

Nancy peeked over Angel's shoulder and watched as his hand moved the pencil across the page in sure, even strokes. His drawing was a copy of the gown executed in sweeping, romantic lines.

"I don't understand," Nancy said. "Isn't sketching a design the first step? Then don't you make a sample from the sketch?"

"Some designers work that way," Angel explained. "But Beau likes to work with the fabric, playing with the texture and weight of the cloth. He drapes the fabric on a dress form or model until the right shape emerges. Then, after the design is complete, I sketch it."

"What are the sketches for?" Nancy asked.

"Promotion pieces, catalogs, and records." Angel pointed to the binders that lined the shelves on one wall. "Those books are filled with sketches of gowns in the Beau Bridal collection."

"There are sandwiches for everyone in the lounge," Beau announced. "We won't have time to break for lunch today."

Angel added a few touches to the sketch, then stood up. "Hungry?" he asked Nancy.

"I could use a sandwich," Nancy said, smiling at the soft-spoken young man. As she followed him down the hall, Nancy pointed to closed doors, and Angel told her what was inside.

"Those two are fitting rooms," he explained. "That's a storage room. Bathroom. And this is our home away from home." The lounge was a small room furnished with two sofas, a table and chairs, a microwave, and a refrigerator. On the table were a platter of sliced meats and cheeses and bowls of rolls, bread, salad, and pickles.

Angel bit into a pickle. "My mother always told me to eat my vegetables," he teased.

Nancy laughed as she made herself a turkey sandwich. "And you'd better stay healthy with the show coming up."

"That's for sure," Angel agreed.

"How long have you worked for Beau?" she asked.

"Almost two years," he answered. "I was hired

when Beau moved into this studio. Before that, he worked out of his apartment with Mrs. Chong and one or two part-time assistants."

"You sketch beautifully," Nancy said. "Do you enjoy your work?"

Angel shrugged. "It gets crazy around here, but I like working in the field. I'm actually trained as a designer." His dark eyes took on a dreamy look as he added, "Beau might include some of my designs in his next collection, which would be a dream come true."

Nancy was about to ask another question when two workers came in, chattering loudly as they pushed toward the food.

"Guess I'd better get back to work," Angel said, heading down the hall with a plate of food.

After Nancy had finished her sandwich, she set off to check out the rest of the studio. The fitting rooms were furnished with a few chairs, thick carpeting, mirrors, and oriental screens.

Then she opened the door to the storage room Angel had pointed out. She could only make out heaps of clutter in the darkness. She switched on the light and found herself in an unfurnished room with exposed studs, laths, and wiring.

Dresses lined the walls. Nancy assumed they were old samples. A fallen dress form lay on the floor, its padded contours sagging, and dusty boxes were stacked against one wall.

Nothing here, Nancy thought, switching off the light. She was about to leave when she heard voices. Realizing that the storage room must back up to Beau's office, she followed the source of the sound and found a crack in the plasterboard on Beau's side.

Pressing her face between the laths, she realized the crack wasn't wide enough to see through. She took a penknife out of her pocket and scraped out a hole only large enough to see through.

She could see Beau talking with Mrs. Chong now.

Twisting the ends of a measuring tape that dangled around her neck, the woman waited while Beau spoke. "About the money for your husband's treatment—" Beau said gently. "I want you to know that I'm still trying, but it's not easy to scrape together six thousand dollars."

"No need," Mrs. Chong said. "We have money."

"So he can have the operation!" Beau sounded cheerful. "What happened? Did the insurance company finally come through?"

"No," Mrs. Chong said. "Medical insurance won't pay for experimental treatment."

"So how did you get the money?" Beau asked.

She pursed her lips. "Here and there. No more problem." She nodded, then marched out of the office in her usual brusque manner.

Nancy moved away from the peephole and thought for a moment in the dark storeroom. Mrs. Chong had mysteriously found money—

and *lots* of it. Did she steal Beau's designs and sell them to Budget to pay for her husband's medical expenses?

Before Nancy could mull that over, she heard a man's voice. Peering through the hole, she saw that Angel had now gone into Beau's office.

"Why are you holding me back?" Angel asked, leaning over Beau's desk. "I've finished samples for two of my designs, and they're ready to show."

Behind the desk, Beau shook his head. "Your designs don't fit in with the overall theme of my spring collection," Beau said. "Next time, we'll work on something together. But for now, I just can't include two dresses that don't work."

Angel's dark eyes glowered as he snatched up his sketches. "It's just not fair," he said. "My designs deserve to be shown—and you know it."

Nancy was amazed at how much more forceful Angel seemed now than he had when they'd talked earlier.

"I'm sorry," Beau said sadly, "but—".

"We've had this conversation before," Angel said, pounding his fist onto the desk. "You better listen to me. You can't ignore me forever." Then he stormed out of the office, slamming the door behind him.

Chapter
Seven

SITTING BACK on the floor, Nancy considered the situation. Angel obviously had a bone to pick with Beau. Would he steal Joanna's gown to further weaken his boss?

Nancy stood up, dusted off her pants, and headed for Beau's office. She found the door open. Head in hands, Beau was sitting, staring at his desktop.

"Got a minute?" she asked from the doorway.

"Only if you've got good news," Beau said.

"I'm afraid not." Nancy went in, closed the door, and sat in the chair opposite Beau's desk. "I've been checking out your setup here. Given the lack of security, I'm surprised you have a sewing machine left in the studio."

Beau groaned. "Is it really that bad?"

Nancy ran down the list of problems from the

63

main lock downstairs to the Dumpster out front. "Anyone who wants to know what you're up to can just dig through that bin," she finished off. "There are bound to be discarded fabric swatches and sketches—enough to allow someone to try to piece together your spring collection."

"But I don't design on paper," Beau said, wearily rubbing the back of his neck.

"Angel mentioned that," Nancy said. "But I imagine that any botched sketches of the finished gowns would end up in the dumpster."

"Nope," Beau insisted. "Angel gets them right every time. He's fabulous."

"Well, that's good news," Nancy said. "At least the sketches aren't sitting in the trash bin out front." Remembering what she'd seen and heard from the storeroom, Nancy added, "What about Mrs. Chong? Does she sketch the gowns, too?"

"No," Beau said. "She's a sample maker. She makes trial versions of my designs. Mrs. Chong can't sketch, but she's a whiz with scissors, needle, and thread."

Despite Beau's affection for his assistants, Nancy reminded herself that they were both prime suspects. "What if Mrs. Chong is the one stealing your designs?" she asked.

Beau frowned. "I'd be shocked. She's worked with me since I set up shop in my apartment."

"How long ago was that?" Nancy asked.

"About five years ago," Beau answered.

His dark eyes were thoughtful as he spoke. "Since I was a kid, I knew I wanted to be a designer. I grew up in an artists' colony in New England, a place full of painters and writers. My parents encouraged my interest in fashion design —even when I poured all my savings into my first line of bridal gowns. And Mrs. Chong has been there from the beginning, supporting me."

"Sometimes people lose track of their loyalties," Nancy said gently.

"Not Mrs. Chong," Beau said. "She can breathe fire when she wants to, but I can't imagine her turning against me."

"But Mrs. Chong was the last person to see Joanna's gown on Sunday night, when she was alone here in the studio," Nancy pointed out. "She also has a key to the vault."

Beau was shaking his head. "She can't sketch. How could she pass on my designs?"

"You said she's a whiz at sewing," Nancy answered. "It sounds as if she could whip up a sample in no time."

With a sigh, Beau leaned back. From his troubled expression, Nancy knew this was difficult for him. "I see your point. Although I don't want to believe Mrs. Chong is stealing from me."

"But she has a strong motive—her husband," Nancy pointed out. "Maybe she got the money for his operation by selling your designs to Budget."

Beau squinted at Nancy. "How did you find

out about her husband's treatment? Mrs. Chong rarely talks about her personal life."

"I've been watching you," Nancy said, going over to the wall to point out the barely visible crack. She explained her discovery in the storage room.

"You were spying on me?" Beau said, pretending to be offended.

Nancy smiled. "You're the one they're stealing from. Doesn't it make sense to figure out how they're doing it?"

"You're right," Beau said. "And don't get me wrong—I appreciate your work."

"I also heard your argument with Angel," said Nancy. "He's upset that you're not using his designs. And he has a key to the vault, too. Do you think he could have stolen Joanna's dress to get back at you?"

Beau scratched his chin thoughtfully. "It's possible—though I don't think he's that mad."

"Think about it," Nancy said. "He does all your sketches and could probably reproduce them in minutes. Angel might be selling your designs to Budget to spoil the reception of your line. If enough of your designs were leaked in advance, there might be a chance that you'd have to use one of his creations in the show."

"I never considered that," Beau said. "Do you think he's the spy?"

"I'm not sure yet," Nancy said. "I still have a few leads to check out."

"In the meantime, I'm going to lay down the law on the use of our security system. Of course, we can't have the alarm system on while we're in here, but we can have the doors locked." He picked up the phone and punched in a number. "And I'm calling the landlord to see about getting a new lock on the door downstairs."

"You may want to wait on that," Nancy said, and Beau quickly cut the line. "I want whoever is stealing this stuff to think it's still safe until we've got the person pegged—with enough evidence to make an arrest."

"Fair enough." Beau hung up the phone, then reached into the top drawer of his desk. "In that case, here's a key to the lobby entrance. If you want to deactivate the alarm at the studio door, just spell out *bridal* on the keypad. I don't know if you plan to be here after hours, but I want you to feel free to come and go as you please."

"Thanks." Nancy stood up and slipped the key in her pocket. "Who else knows the code to the lock outside the studio?"

"Angel, Mrs. Chong, and I—same as the vault," Beau said. "One of us always sets the alarm and lock when we leave at night." Beau checked his watch and pushed away from his desk. "I'd better get back to the workroom. I've got some runway models coming in for a fitting. We hire a troop of models for our seasonal shows."

Nancy nodded. "And I should check on Bess."

"Miss Petite Elite?" Beau smiled. "I'm glad she's modeling for us. She really makes the new line come alive."

"I feel like a kid in a candy store," Bess said, twirling around. As she moved, the gathered skirt of her gown billowed out gracefully.

Nancy had found Bess in the vault with Angel. "We need you to try on two more gowns," Angel said, pushing through the dresses on one of the wall racks. He stopped when he revealed a rust-colored dress made of suede. "This is one of Beau's wilder designs—it's backless, and it's the first time he's used suede for an evening dress."

"It does stand out from his other designs," Bess said.

Nancy reached out and ran her hand along the gown. She could imagine herself wearing this dress as she and Ned spun around on the dance floor. "I love it," she said. As she lifted the dress, she noticed a dark grate on the wall behind it.

"Wait a minute," Nancy said, sliding the gown along the rack to clear a space. The grid, about three feet wide and two feet high, covered an air vent. "I didn't know this was here."

"Didn't you notice it yesterday when you checked out the vault?" Bess asked.

Nancy shook her head. "I asked Beau to check for any cracks or holes on this wall. I guess he didn't think the vent counted." She ran her fingers over the metal grate.

"Wow," Bess said. "Do you think—"

Nancy was already one step ahead of her. "Will you help me pry off this cover?" Nancy asked Angel. "The screws have been removed."

"Sure," he said, digging his fingers into the edge of the frame. "We'll probably need a screwdriver to get some leverage—" He tugged, and all at once the vent cover popped off.

"It must have been loose," Bess said as Angel placed the grate on the floor.

"Or maybe it was removed recently." Nancy peered into the dark opening that led to a wide air shaft. "Maybe the person who stole Joanna's gown came in this way." She pulled her penlight out of her pocket. "I'll check it out."

"Be careful," Angel said. "I don't know where this thing leads."

Inside the dark shaft, Nancy gripped her penlight in one fist as she moved forward on her hands and knees. The walls of the vent were coated with dust, but a trail was worn clear on the bottom, as if someone had crawled through the space recently.

Did the thief sneak in this way, grab the dress, and drag it back out through the vent?

Nancy reached a place where another shaft intersected. Should I turn? she wondered. Then the beam of the penlight revealed the trail worn through the dust. It led straight ahead. She crept forward.

The beam of light bounced over a jagged seam

in the vent, and a tiny kernel glistened there. Nancy paused and turned the light on the object. It was a seed pearl. Could it be like the ones on Joanna's dress?

Excited, Nancy picked up the pearl and continued on, following the clean trail. She began to hear muffled voices, then noticed light streaming in through a grid ahead of her.

The thief must have come in through this opening, she thought, pressing against the grate. It took a couple of shoves, but finally the vent cover gave way.

The grate crashed to the floor, startling a roomful of workers who spun around to face her. Nancy peered out into the sunny workroom and saw the startled expressions of Beau, Mrs. Chong, and the design team.

Just a few feet from the vent, Mrs. Chong wheeled defensively, her face fierce. She raised her hand over her head, ready to attack the intruder.

Light glinted off the gold-handled scissors in Mrs. Chong's hand as the razor-sharp points rushed toward Nancy.

Chapter

Eight

"STOP!" Nancy backed deeper into the shaft, covering her head with her arms.

"It's okay, Mrs. Chong," Beau shouted, rushing forward. He grabbed the woman around the shoulders, pulling her backward so that she stabbed at thin air.

"I thought . . ." Mrs. Chong eyed Nancy suspiciously, then relaxed. She replaced the scissors in a special box, lining them up beside the rest of the collection with distinctive gold handles, then turned to Nancy. "What are you, a crazy girl?" she snapped. "Popping out of the walls, scaring people out of their minds."

"I'm sure there's a reasonable explanation," Beau said, stepping toward Nancy. "Need a hand?"

Beau helped to pull Nancy out. "Thanks," she said, brushing the dust off her clothes.

Just then Bess and Angel rushed in from the hall, looking nervous until they spotted Nancy. "You're here!" Bess said, relieved. "I was hoping you were the cause of all the noise."

"We were waiting for you to return to the vault," Angel explained. "When we called into the air shaft and got no answer, Bess started to worry. Are you okay?"

"I'm fine," Nancy assured them. "A little dusty, but it was worth it." She held up the seed pearl, then passed it to Beau. "I found this inside the air shaft."

Beau held the tiny pearl in the palm of his hand and studied it. "It looks like one of the seed pearls from Joanna Rockwell's gown," he said. "But how did it get into the air shaft?"

"The dust in the air shaft was worn clean in a single trail, as if someone had crawled through it recently," Nancy explained. "I followed the clean trail to this vent. There's a good chance that Joanna's gown was removed from the vault through that vent."

"It did pop right out when you gave it a shove," Beau said, picking up the grate. Peering over his shoulder, Nancy saw that the screws had been removed from this vent cover, too.

Nancy turned to Mrs. Chong. "The other night when you heard the noise in here, which room were you working in?"

"Sewing room," the woman said, pointing a bony finger at the tiny room on the other side of the workroom.

"That noise might have been the thief, covering his tracks," Nancy said, taking the vent cover and shoving it into place with a thud.

"That means the gown could have been stolen by an outsider," Beau said, smiling. Nancy suspected he was relieved to think that his employees were in the clear.

"It's possible," Nancy said, knowing that the gown still could have been stolen by one of his employees. Angel or even Mrs. Chong might have dragged the gown through the shaft to divert attention from themselves.

An hour later the studio had settled back to its usual hectic pace. Nancy needed some time in the studio to observe the routine so she had agreed to spend the afternoon in the workroom, running errands for Beau, Angel, and Mrs. Chong.

In one corner Bess stood still as a statue, modeling while Eleni marked the rust-colored suede dress for alterations.

Beau was working with the model named Isis. Nancy watched as he draped sheer chiffon over her arms, fashioning sleeves. Absorbed in his work, Beau seemed to have blocked out everything else.

An assistant came in to tell Beau that Joanna

and her maid of honor had arrived. Nancy followed him into the fitting room to greet them.

"Hi," Joanna said, standing up and flashing them a smile. "Nancy, this is Elizabeth Baker, my maid of honor."

"Call me Liz," the tall, rangy girl said. She had long, carrot-colored hair that was held back with two tortoise-shell combs.

"Your dress is finished, Liz," Beau told her. "You can try it on, just to make sure you're happy with it."

"Great!" Liz said. "But first I'd like to see Joanna's number-two gown."

"No problem. We'll retrieve both dresses from the vault," Beau said, motioning an assistant to follow him as he left the room.

As soon as the door closed, Joanna turned to Nancy. "Any leads on my gown?" she asked.

Nancy showed her the seed pearl she'd found in the air shaft.

"That must be from my gown!" Joanna said excitedly.

Just then there was a knock on the door, and Beau entered carrying two gowns. "For Liz," he said, hanging an emerald green satin gown on one rack. "And, Joanna," he said, forcing a smile, "careful trying yours on. Some of the seams are just basted. I'll be back in a few minutes to see how you're doing." Then he left the fitting room.

Joanna and Liz ducked behind two oriental screens and quickly changed into the gowns.

"This is perfect," Liz said, smoothing the satin folds over her hips.

"Oh, Lizzy, you look great!" Joanna said as she turned to look at her own reflection and frowned. "Too bad the rest of the bridal party isn't here." Turning to Nancy, she added, "Two of my bridesmaids had last-minute emergencies and won't even arrive until Friday morning. They're going to miss tomorrow night's rehearsal dinner!"

"Not a big deal," Liz said, trying to calm her friend. "We'll make do without them."

"But it's going to throw off the procession," Joanna insisted. "Everyone will be confused."

"If it would help, Bess and I could take their places at the rehearsal," Nancy offered. "Then we'll clue them in when they arrive."

"Would you?" Joanna's green eyes widened hopefully. "We're rehearsing at St. Patrick's Cathedral on Fifth Avenue. Sam's brothers will be there—and they're so cute! We start at five, then we're off to dinner at the Russian Tea Room."

There was a knock at the door, and Nancy opened it to find Beau.

"How's it going?" he asked.

"I'm in love"—Liz twirled around—"with my dress!"

Beau smiled. "It's always nice to have a satisfied client." He knelt beside Joanna and rearranged the bustle of her gown. "With a few tucks, this should be fine, too. Though I'm not giving up on the gown with your mother's pearls."

"Thanks for whipping this up for me, Beau," Joanna said sincerely. "I know that rumors are flying about the gown Mimi made for me."

Beau tensed for a moment, then nodded. "I saw Delia's report this morning."

"But I haven't spoken to Mimi for months," Joanna told him. "I want you to know that I'm going to stick with you and wear one of your designs. No matter what Mimi does!"

"Thanks," Beau told Joanna. "Most clients aren't so loyal. You've been an angel."

"Mimi is persistent," Liz added. "Can you believe that she had an invitation to her show hand-delivered to Joanna this morning?" Liz snorted. "That woman doesn't give up."

"An invitation?" Beau said, glancing at Nancy. "There's your chance."

"Don't worry. I'm not going," Joanna said.

"But you should," Beau insisted.

Quickly Nancy explained that she and Bess needed a way into Mimi Piazza's studio. "She might have something to do with stealing Beau's designs. Maybe she even knows something about your gown."

"What?" Joanna and Liz said in unison.

"Mimi has always been a rival of mine," Beau said. "She'd love to see my business crumble, and considering the way things are going, she may get her wish."

"I really need a way to check her out," Nancy said.

"Well, then, I guess we'll be attending her show on Thursday morning," Joanna said firmly. "I'll call her studio and make sure that you and Bess are added to the guest list."

"Modeling is a lot of hard work," Bess said. She rolled her shoulders and rubbed the back of her neck.

"Not all glamour and smiles?" Nancy teased.

Outside the huge windows of the workroom, night had descended over New York City. The studio had emptied out, except for Beau, Angel, and Mrs. Chong.

"You've been a big help, Bess," Beau told her.

"Thanks," Bess said, smiling. "I love being around all these gorgeous gowns. Though you guys do put in long days."

"We'll be here for a few more hours," Angel explained to the girls as he sketched a gown that hung on a dress form in front of him.

Mrs. Chong barreled through the room, Joanna's replacement gown in her arms. "Sewing all night," she complained. "I sew in my sleep." She marched into her little sewing room.

"She's got a lot on her mind," Beau said as if apologizing for Mrs. Chong.

"I guess we'll head out," Nancy said. "We'll see

77

you tomorrow after our—appointment." She didn't want to be more specific within earshot of Angel and Mrs. Chong.

"So long," Beau said, disappearing into his office as the girls headed out to the elevator.

"What's the plan for tomorrow?" Bess asked as the elevator doors opened and the girls stepped inside.

"We have an appointment at Budget Fashions at nine-thirty," Nancy said, explaining how Jill's assistant had vouched for them. "After she got the okay from Jill, she set the whole thing up. She told Budget that we're in a training program at Mitchell's." Nancy and Bess crossed the lobby and opened the door into the cool autumn night.

"Let's walk a bit and then hail a cab," she said. Just then, she heard a squeaking noise above them. Glancing up, she saw that it was just a window being forced open.

A second later Nancy noticed a dark figure edging out from the opening above them. Suddenly it was falling—plunging toward the sidewalk.

It was going to hit Nancy and Bess!

Chapter

Nine

LOOK OUT!" Nancy shouted, at the same time throwing her arms around Bess and sweeping them both back toward the front door.

They landed on the cold cement threshold just as Nancy heard the thud of the body hitting the pavement nearby.

"Ouch!" Bess said, sitting up and rubbing her elbow. "What happened?"

Nancy steeled herself to check on the body. For a moment she thought her eyes were playing tricks on her, then she sighed with relief. On the sidewalk, in the spot where she and Bess had been standing, lay a dress form clothed in a muslin gown, its metal stand bent from the fall.

"That's a relief," Nancy said, brushing herself off as she nodded at the dressmaker's dummy. "I thought that was a person falling out of the window."

Bess grimaced. "I'm glad you were wrong," she said, "but that thing still came within a foot of clobbering us."

Nancy looked up at the building just in time to see the huge window three stories up being slammed shut. "It came from the fourth floor," she said, running through the floor plan in her mind. "From the workroom of Beau's studio."

"Could it have fallen accidentally?" Bess asked, picking the dummy up.

"That's doubtful," Nancy said, frowning. "Let's take this upstairs and find out what happened."

Beau was surprised to see Nancy and Bess at the door with one of his slightly battered dress forms. He summoned Angel and Mrs. Chong, who listened intently as Nancy described the incident.

"But who could have done it?" Angel asked, his dark eyes concerned. "The three of us are the only ones left in the studio. I was putting gowns back into the vault, and Mrs. Chong was in the sewing room."

"I was on the phone in my office," Beau said, frowning. "I'm glad you girls didn't get hurt."

Mrs. Chong said to Nancy, "I think you are bad luck. You arrive, and a gown disappears. Dummies jump out of windows. Very bad luck."

"Mrs. Chong," Beau said patiently, "Nancy is trying to help us."

"Mmm." She shook her head. "No help so far."

Nancy studied the faces of Beau's right-hand employees. Angel seemed genuinely concerned. Mrs. Chong looked as if she wouldn't have minded if Nancy and Bess had been flattened by the dummy. She couldn't tell who had tossed it out the window.

The only thing she could be sure of was that one of them wanted her off the case.

On Wednesday morning Nancy and Bess took a cab from Eloise Drew's apartment to the showroom of Budget Fashions. The driver pulled up in front of a dingy building with half a dozen loading docks stretching out from the structure. Workers milled around, loading and unloading trucks.

"I hope I look like a buyer-in-training," Bess said, tying a printed scarf over her teal blue jacket.

"You look great," Nancy said as she paid the cab driver. After she stepped out, she straightened the skirt of her plaid wool suit.

They found the showroom, a large area that reminded Nancy of a boutique. From the clothes that hung on the walls and on racks, she could see that Budget Fashions didn't limit its business to bridal gowns. They also sold women's sportswear.

Nancy's eyes were immediately drawn to a pants and vest ensemble made from fire-engine red leather. Near it hung Budget's Safari Sportswear line, with pants, blazers, and jackets printed in tiger stripes and leopard spots.

A short, round woman with auburn hair looked up from a computer printout at the front counter, which served as a reception area. "What can I do for you today, ladies?"

"We're the trainees from Mitchell's," Nancy said, introducing herself and Bess.

"Ah, yes," the woman said. "Your appointment is with me, Katrina Ivanovich. I'm in charge of sales here at Budget. All the women's buyers at Mitchell's know me," she bragged. "They come to Budget when they want a designer look at a third of the price. Now, what can I show you?"

"We'd love to see how your operation works," Nancy said, trying to stick as close to the truth as possible. "Our main purpose is to learn."

"Fashion is my passion," Bess said, her blue eyes sparkling.

"I see," Katrina said. "Is there an area of women's wear you have a particular interest in?"

"Bridal and formal wear," Nancy answered.

"Then we should start over here." Katrina rounded the counter and led the girls to the far corner of the showroom.

Nancy passed a faceless mannequin swathed in a bridal gown, then turned to a rack of evening gowns. She flipped past three gowns until she came to the pale blue sample they'd seen at Mitchell's—the knockoff of Beau's design.

Bess gave her a knowing look, then said, "There's so much to choose from. Who designs your evening wear?"

"Oh, we pick up designs here and there. Our best-selling merchandise is inspired by top designers," Katrina said evasively. "Everything is manufactured and shipped from this building."

"Is there any way we can see what goes on behind the scenes?" Nancy suggested. "It must be fascinating."

Bess's eyes lit up as she played her role to the hilt. "That would be the highlight of our trip!" she said hopefully.

"We usually don't take anyone beyond the showroom," Katrina said, checking her watch. "But I guess I could make an exception for you."

Nancy smiled as the older woman led them through a door and down a narrow corridor. If she could find a way to sneak off by herself, she might be able to find some record of who had sold Beau's designs to Budget.

"Here's our shipping department," Katrina explained as the girls stepped into the cavernous room with rolling doors open to the street. Trucks were parked in some of the loading bays, and workers bustled around, moving boxes and rolling racks of finished clothes.

Their next stop was the cutting room on the first floor, where the pace was fast. The pace on the second floor was even more rushed, though. There, dozens of sewing machines were lined up, operated by an army of workers who assembled the pieces. On the third floor, huge steam presses hissed as workers pressed the garments for shipping.

As she followed Katrina, Nancy waited for an excuse to slip away, but the woman watched the girls like a mother hen.

Their tour ended back at the showroom where it had begun. When Katrina was called away for a moment the girls wandered back to the evening gown display. Nancy leaned close to Bess and whispered, "Ask her about the blue dress."

"She'd never let on who sold them the design," Bess said under her breath.

"She might tell *you*," Nancy pointed out.

Bess frowned but quickly snapped back to her cheerful mode when Katrina returned.

"What else can I show you?" the woman asked.

"Well," Bess said, combing through some of the dresses on the rack. "As you know, I've been studying different designers' work. If I guess whose designs some of these dresses are based on, would you tell me if I'm right?"

Katrina looked around the showroom, which

was quiet at the moment. "All right," she agreed. "I'll do it for you—and Mitchell's."

Bess turned to the wedding gown on the mannequin and smiled. "This design must have been inspired by Dona Vaquez."

"That's right," Katrina said, nodding. "What about this?" she asked, holding up a black sequined gown with a velvet bolero.

"Jacques Loire?" Bess asked.

"No, dear," Katrina said, wagging a finger at Bess. "It's Anton Strauss."

Nancy decided it was time to jump in. "What about this dress?" she asked, holding up the blue polyester skirt of the knockoff from Beau's collection.

"That looks like a Beau Winston gown," Bess said, ready to gauge Katrina's reaction.

The saleswoman shook her head. "You wouldn't be able to guess that one. We bought that design from a free-lance designer, a new talent you've probably never heard of. His name is Angel Ortiz."

Chapter

Ten

"ANGEL?" Bess responded, blinking in surprise.

"Ah, you've heard of him," Katrina said as if pleased.

"I—I," Bess stuttered. "I was just thinking that—that it's a great name for a designer."

Nancy barely registered the conversation. Her mind was backtracking, going over the clues that should have pointed to Angel. Suddenly she couldn't wait to get back to the studio and warn Beau.

"What about this one?" Katrina's eyebrows wiggled as she held up another gown.

But Nancy had lost interest in the game. The sooner she and Bess could get out of there, the better. Pretending to have another appointment, Nancy cut the conversation short and thanked

Katrina. Within minutes, the girls were in a cab on their way to Beau's studio.

"Angel!" Bess repeated. "A big part of the mystery is solved. But he's the last person I suspected. He seems so quiet and sweet."

"But he is an aspiring designer," Nancy said, telling Bess about the argument she'd watched between Angel and Beau. "Angel thinks Beau is holding him back. He may be selling off Beau's designs for revenge."

"Or maybe he's using the designs to get ahead," Bess pointed out. "The people at Budget think Angel designed that blue gown. If his name is heard often enough, he could gain acceptance in the industry."

"I should have guessed it was Angel," Nancy said. "He draws all of Beau's sketches, so it would be easy for him to whip up copies."

"Do you think Angel was the one who tossed that dummy down on us last night?" Bess asked.

"It had to be," Nancy said. "He said he was in the vault, but he must have been lying."

"It's creepy," Bess said as the cab turned toward Beau's studio. "He was willing to hurt or maybe kill us, just to get you off the case."

Nancy nodded thoughtfully. "A strong reaction for a guy who just wants his designs shown."

"Wait a second," Bess said, studying her friend's face. "I smell an idea brewing. You don't like Angel's motive."

Nancy nodded. "Even if he stole the designs

and Joanna's wedding gown, it's not enough to kill us over," she said.

"Do you think he's working for someone else?"

"It's possible," Nancy said. "I know Angel must be the design thief. What I need to find out is if he has an accomplice—someone like Mimi Piazza or Michael Rockwell."

"What are you going to do now?" asked Bess.

"I need to talk to Beau. I'm sure he'll fire Angel on the spot," Nancy said. "The fact that he tried to hit us with a dress form is a matter for the police—if we report it."

"Why don't we call the police now and have him arrested?" Bess asked as the cab pulled up in front of Beau's studio.

Nancy considered the idea as she pulled several bills out of her purse and handed them to the driver. "I don't think there's enough evidence to convict him of throwing that dress form at us," she said. "As for the design theft, fashion espionage isn't usually prosecuted."

Bess climbed out of the cab and slammed the door behind her. "I don't like it," she said, staring up at the building grimly.

"Don't worry," Nancy said, taking her friend by the arm and guiding her toward the lobby. "The minute Beau finds out what's been going on, Angel will be out of here."

Beau was nowhere to be found, though. "You just missed him," Eleni told Nancy when the girls went into the workroom after checking Beau's office. "He went to the Plaza Hotel to make arrangements for next week's show."

Nancy noticed Bess biting her lip nervously.

"Don't look so worried," Eleni said, sewing a tiny pearlized button into place on an ice pink gown. "He'll be back this afternoon."

"Maybe we should go to lunch and come back later," Bess suggested. "We can—"

"No, no, no," Mrs. Chong interrupted. She took Bess by the hand and pulled her toward one of the fitting rooms. "Eat here. You need to have final fittings on your gowns. And you," she added, eyeing Nancy, "we'll find something to keep you from climbing the walls."

Nancy was pushing up the sleeves of her sweater when she saw Angel standing in the doorway, sketchbook in his arms.

"Nobody gets out alive," he said wryly, adding, "at least not during the week before a show."

Forcing a smile, Nancy nodded, though she felt uncomfortable now that she knew Angel was the one who was betraying Beau. She followed Bess into the fitting room just before Mrs. Chong shoved the ice pink gown at her, then charged out, slamming the door behind her.

"Suddenly modeling has lost its glamour," Bess said, unzipping the pink gown.

"Listen, I'll try to reach Beau at the Plaza," Nancy promised her friend. "In the meantime, just act normal. If Angel figures out that we know he's the thief, there's no telling what he might do."

The afternoon dragged.

Bess tried to avoid Angel, but every time she had a final fitting, he was at her side, sketching the gown.

Nancy had tried to reach Beau, but he never answered the page at the Plaza. She resigned herself to fetching notions, removing pins, and unrolling bolts of lace for Mrs. Chong.

All the while, Nancy kept thinking of Joanna's gown. Had Angel stolen that, too? Since he had a key to the vault, it didn't seem likely that he'd have dragged it through the air shaft. Still, he might have used the air shaft to draw suspicion away from himself.

Nancy then recalled the surprise on Angel's face the day before when the vent cover had popped off so quickly. Was he acting? Or had Joanna's wedding gown been stolen by someone else?

If Angel is the thief, I hope he has the Rockwell gown stashed in a safe place, Nancy thought, crossing her fingers. Maybe Beau would give him a chance to make amends by returning the gown. If things fall into place, Nancy told herself, two crimes could be solved by the end of the day.

"Enough lace!" Mrs. Chong snapped, interrupting Nancy's thoughts. The older woman measured and cut off the yardage she needed, then pointed to two small boxes on the floor of the workroom. "Those go to storage," she said.

Nancy saw that the boxes contained leftover buttons and spools of trim. She picked them up and carried them to the storage room next to Beau's office.

The shelves were cluttered, but she managed to clear a space beside a plastic bin of silk flowers. Nancy was on her way out when she heard someone talking in Beau's office. He must be back, she thought, moving to the hole in the wall to check.

When she peered through the peephole, she saw only Angel. He was sitting at Beau's desk, talking so quietly on the phone that she could barely make out what he was saying.

Holding her breath, Nancy concentrated on listening.

"The way I see it, *I'm* the one who's taking all the chances," he muttered. "You're locked up all safe and sound behind your castle walls."

Castle walls? Nancy mused. Who was Angel talking to?

"I'm losing patience. We have to talk—no, not now!" he insisted. "Meet me here tonight at ten-thirty. No one else will be around."

Angel listened in silence for a moment, then snapped, "I'm not in this alone. Meet me here—unless you want to see yourself on the next installment of 'Fashion Flash'!"

Chapter

Eleven

I'M NOT IN this alone."

Angel's words rang through Nancy's mind as she watched him hang up the phone and leave Beau's office. So he *was* working with a partner. But who?

From what he'd said, she knew Angel's partner had to be involved in the fashion industry, which seemed to rule out Michael Rockwell.

Nancy was also surprised that Angel had told his partner to meet him at the studio. With Beau's show next week, wouldn't Beau and Mrs. Chong be working late, too?

The mystery deepened when Nancy returned to the workroom to find Mrs. Chong buttoning her coat. "Tell Mr. Beau I'm gone for the day," she ordered Angel. "You covering tonight?"

He nodded and assured her, "I'll be here."

Nancy checked her watch as Mrs. Chong marched out. It was only four-thirty. "What's going on?" she asked Angel. "Mrs. Chong doesn't usually leave so early."

"You'll have to ask Beau," Angel told her. "I've been sworn to secrecy." He picked up his sketch-pad and went down the hall toward the vault.

Nancy turned to Bess, who was modeling a navy sequined gown for Eleni. "You'd better change back into your own clothes," Nancy told her friend. "If we don't leave soon, we're going to be late for the wedding rehearsal."

"But Beau still isn't back from the Plaza," Bess pointed out. "I wonder what's keeping him."

"The details of a show are endless," Eleni volunteered. "He's got to check out the space and make sure the runway can be seen by all members of the audience. He has to work with the hotel on seating arrangements and security. Then there's the music and the little extras that turn a show into a publicity event. Last year we gave an orchid to each guest. I don't know what Beau has planned for this year."

"I hate to leave without speaking to him," Nancy said, "but we can't let Joanna down."

"Can I give him a message?" Eleni offered. "Or I'll give you Beau's home phone number so you can leave a message on his machine," she suggested to Nancy. "He checks his messages every hour or so."

While Bess changed, Nancy called and left a

message for Beau on his machine. "We've got to talk—it's urgent," she said. "I'm going to be moving around, so I'll try you later."

With no time to spare, Nancy and Bess left the studio and waved down a cab. It was just a few minutes after five when the taxi pulled up in front of St. Patrick's Cathedral.

"I'd forgotten how grand this place is," Bess said as she leaned forward to pay the driver.

Nancy stepped out of the cab and looked up at the cathedral's twin Gothic spires. Tourists streamed in and out through one set of wide doors tucked beneath graceful arches.

Inside, the girls had to maneuver past more sightseers. There, past a stand of candles glittering in red glass, Nancy finally spotted Sam Hollingsworth standing in the aisle with a group of men.

"Hi, Sam," Nancy said, smiling as she approached the guys. "How's it going?"

"Don't ask!" he said, rubbing his temples. "We just got word that Joanna's father is stuck in Chicago. He flew there for a business meeting, and now the airport is fogged in. He's not going to make it back tonight so Joanna's in a tizzy."

Following the direction of his gaze, Nancy spotted Joanna standing at the side of the altar. She was talking with Liz Baker and a priest, a young man dressed in a black shirt with a clerical collar. When Nancy and Bess joined them, Joanna apologized.

"I'm sorry you two made the trip for nothing," she said, her green eyes wide.

"You mean you're canceling the rehearsal?" Bess asked.

"We might as well," Joanna said. "What's the use? Half the people in the bridal party aren't here."

"That's a bit of an exaggeration," Liz pointed out, trying to calm her friend.

"Well," Joanna said sadly, "I'm the only member of the Rockwell family here, and it sure doesn't feel right. Maybe this whole wedding just wasn't meant to be."

Nancy was struck by Joanna's statement. Her gown had been stolen. Her father, who had suggested canceling the wedding, couldn't make it to the rehearsal. Her brother had refused to be in the bridal party. The Rockwells were hardly surrounding Joanna with warmth and support during this hectic time.

"Don't let anyone leave," Nancy whispered to Bess. "I'll be right back."

Motioning for Sam to join her, Nancy found a quiet place in one of the side aisles. "Do you know how to get in touch with Tyler?" she asked him. When he nodded, she added, "You have to call him to see if he'll take Michael Rockwell's place for the rehearsal. Joanna feels as if her family has let her down, and right now Tyler's the only person who can change that."

"Tyler's not the most reliable guy in the

world," Sam admitted, his blue eyes thoughtful. "But he and Joanna used to be close when they were kids. I'll give it a shot."

He strode down the aisle and led Nancy to an area in the back of the cathedral with a gift shop, lavatories, and pay phones. While Sam phoned Tyler, Nancy called Beau's studio but was told he hadn't returned yet. As Nancy thanked the assistant and hung up, she began to worry that something had happened to Beau.

Her attention was diverted when Sam hung up the phone and flashed her a grin. "He's coming," he said. "I had to twist his arm, but finally he agreed. He'll be here in a few minutes."

Back at the altar, Nancy met Sam's two younger brothers, Matt and Larry. Lean, athletic guys with warm smiles, they were joking around with Joanna, trying to cheer her up.

"What happened?" Matt teased, his head thrown back to take in the huge vaulted ceiling of the cathedral. "Couldn't find a place bigger than this?"

Ten minutes later the bridal party was sitting in two pews, listening to the priest describe the ceremony. Tyler walked in just then. Joanna seemed startled at first, but then she jumped out of her seat and danced into the aisle to give her brother a big hug.

"What are you doing here?" she asked.

"Taking Dad's place," he said nonchalantly. "Someone's got to represent the Rockwells."

Joanna's face was beaming when the priest politely asked, "Are we ready to continue?"

With a giggle and a nod, Joanna slid into her pew, pulling her brother along beside her.

After the priest finished the instructions, everyone but Sam and the best man assembled at the back of the cathedral to practice the bridal march.

"Gentlemen, you set the pace," the priest instructed. "Not too fast, but not the walk of a condemned man. This is a happy occasion."

Nancy was paired with Sam's brother, Larry Hollingsworth. He had short, auburn hair and a fun sense of humor. "Ready to rock 'n' roll?" Larry asked, extending his arm.

Smiling, Nancy linked her arm through his. "I'm just your partner for the day," she told him, explaining that she and Bess were filling in for two bridesmaids who wouldn't arrive until Friday.

"You mean I don't get to keep you?" he teased.

"Ladies, remember that you'll be carrying baskets of flowers," the priest said as organ music filled the air and the bridal march began.

Bess sighed. "I love this stuff," she said, reaching up to take Matt's arm. A moment later they were strolling down the aisle.

As she walked beside Larry, Nancy felt relieved that the rehearsal was going on as planned. Michael Rockwell's disapproving face flashed through her mind, and she wondered if her father had uncovered any information about the billionaire. I need to call and check in with Dad, she thought.

After more than an hour of rehearsing, the bridal party piled into three stretch limousines outside the cathedral.

Their next stop was the Russian Tea Room, a restaurant in a narrow building next door to Carnegie Hall. Inside, the bold red, green, and gold decor reminded Nancy of Christmas.

"My mother used to bring me here for lunch when I was a little girl," Joanna told Nancy and Bess.

"Listen," Tyler said, turning to his sister. "I have to get going if I want to make my seven-thirty call for our eight o'clock curtain."

"That's right!" Joanna exclaimed. "I almost forgot. It's the last preview before tomorrow's big opening."

Tyler frowned, then added, "It's no big deal. Dad's not coming. You'll be there, though, right?"

"Sam and I both will be," Joanna promised, then turned to Nancy and Bess. "You guys are welcome to come if you're free."

"If it's for the opening of Tyler's show, we'll make sure we are," Bess said, smiling.

"No big deal," Tyler said, shrugging. For a minute Nancy wondered why he was trying so hard to downplay the importance of his off-Broadway debut.

"Thanks for coming through for me at the rehearsal today," Joanna told her brother. "Isn't there any way I can convince you to be an usher?"

Tyler shook his head. "Sorry, Sis, but I just can't fall in line like a good little soldier and take Dad's orders."

"Can't you set aside your feelings about Dad —just until the wedding is over?" Joanna pleaded. "Can't you do it for *me?*"

Frowning, Tyler zipped up his leather jacket and shoved his hands in the pockets. "I wish I could," he muttered, then cut through the crowd toward the door.

As Nancy watched him leave, she felt sorry for Joanna. Tyler's feud with Michael Rockwell was bound to put a damper on the wedding.

The wedding party settled in at one long table headed by Sam's parents, the hosts of the dinner. The best man, one of Sam's racing buddies named Chase, delivered a humorous toast to the bride and groom. Then the waiters served borscht soup and platters of buttery chicken Kiev.

Around nine o'clock, Nancy went to a pay phone and called Beau's studio. Angel answered. He told her that Beau wasn't expected back at all that night.

What's going on? Nancy wondered.

She called Beau's home number and left a message: "If you can, meet us on the street outside your studio at ten-fifteen tonight," Nancy said. "Whatever you do, don't let anyone see you, and don't go inside!"

"We're not going to make it in time," Nancy said to Bess, checking her watch as the cab lurched forward then stopped for pedestrians. It was almost ten-thirty. The cab was stalled in traffic. It looked as if they were going to miss their chance to discover who Angel's partner was.

"Where did all this traffic come from?" Bess asked the driver.

"We have to cut through the theater district, and the Broadway shows are just ending," he explained, rolling to a stop at a red light.

"We should have left earlier," Bess told Nancy. "But I was having so much fun. Joanna's friends know how to have a good time, and Sam's brothers are so cute. Not to mention all that delicious Russian food."

Staring out the window, Nancy checked the street sign. They were four blocks from Beau's studio, but with the traffic, they'd make better time on foot. "We'll walk the rest of the way," she said as she paid the driver.

Bess climbed out of the cab, then looked down at her flats. "Good thing I didn't wear heels," she said as the girls ran down the street.

By the time they reached the block where

Beau's studio was located, it was already ten-forty. From the street Nancy noticed that the studio lights were on, though Beau was nowhere to be seen.

"I told him to keep a low profile," Nancy muttered. "I wonder if he's here." As she walked, she peered into the shadowed entryway of each building, looking for the designer.

"No sign of Beau," Bess said breathlessly as they reached the front door.

"Let's go on up to the studio," Nancy said. "If we're quiet, we may be able to catch Angel and his partner off guard." She unlocked the lobby door, then motioned Bess to move toward the stairs. "They might hear the elevator," she whispered as they started up the steps.

When they reached the fourth floor, Nancy went over to the electronic keypad beside the door to press in the code to disarm the lock. The light was off, which meant the alarm wasn't on and the door wasn't locked.

She held a finger to her lips, reminding Bess to be quiet. Then she pushed open the studio door and stepped into the reception area.

Dead silence filled the air. Where were they? Nancy wondered as she stole through the outer room. Bess followed, moving carefully to keep from making a sound.

The door to the workroom was open, and a shaft of light spilled onto the floor of the reception area. Nancy's senses tingled in warning. It was too quiet. Something was wrong.

She pressed herself against the wall near the doorway, then peered inside.

A man's body lay facedown on the floor in a pool of dark red blood. Nancy's eyes darted to his face. "It's Angel," she whispered in shock.

Chapter

Twelve

BESS JOINED NANCY in the doorway, then shrank back in horror. "Someone killed him!" she gasped.

Nancy moved into the doorway to survey the scene. From the looks of the body and the amount of blood, it appeared that Angel had been dead for a few minutes at least.

Mrs. Chong's scissors, with their gold handles, were sunk deep in Angel's back. The wooden scissors box was open, and the other scissors were sprawled haphazardly in it. Everything else in the workroom seemed to be in place. There was no sign of a struggle, so Nancy had to assume the killer had taken Angel by surprise.

"I'm calling the police," Bess said. She took a deep breath to regain her composure, then picked up the phone on the desk in the reception area. "There's been a murder," she said, her voice shaking slightly as she gave the address.

When Nancy stepped into the workroom, Bess hung up the phone and called after her, "Where are you going? The killer might be in there!"

"I don't think the person who did this stuck around," Nancy said. A swatch of blue fabric lay on the floor near Angel's body. Not wanting to disturb the evidence, Nancy didn't touch it, but she saw it was a folded piece of fabric with dark blue lace trim around the edge.

It's a handkerchief, she thought, not a fabric sample. The handkerchief was stained with blood. Did it belong to Angel? Or had the killer dropped it accidentally? From the looks of the dainty piece of cloth, Nancy suspected that it belonged to a woman. Suddenly a picture of Mimi Piazza formed in her mind. Didn't Mimi favor tailored suits accented with a dainty hankie?

Maybe Mimi was working with Angel, Nancy thought. Maybe this hankie is the clue that will tie Mimi to the murder! She'd make sure that the police didn't miss this bit of evidence.

Within minutes two uniformed police officers had arrived at the studio. Nancy and Bess were sitting in the small reception area, talking with the female officer, when Beau arrived.

"What's going on?" he asked.

"Beau!" Bess said, sighing with relief. "We were worried about you."

Nancy was overjoyed that Beau was all right. He looked tired, though. His eyes were rimmed with red, and his usually neat hair looked slightly disheveled.

"It's Angel," Nancy said, stepping into Beau's path so that he couldn't walk into the workroom. "He's dead—stabbed with a pair of Mrs. Chong's scissors."

Beau's face registered shock, then horror. "I can't believe what I'm hearing," he said.

Just then three men in suits appeared at the door. The female officer greeted them and pointed them to the body. Two men carried large briefcases into the workroom, while a tall, portly man with salt-and-pepper hair stayed behind.

"I need to go inside and brief the guys from our crime-scene unit," the female officer explained. "They'll collect samples and dust everything for fingerprints." She nodded at the tall man, adding, "This is Detective Noonan. He'll be handling this homicide."

"There's a handkerchief on the floor by the body," Nancy pointed out. "It may be important."

"I'll make sure they get it," the officer said. Then she ducked into the workroom.

While Beau took several deep breaths to calm himself, Nancy introduced herself and Bess to

Detective Noonan. "And this is Beau Winston," she said. "He brought Bess and me into his studio to find out who was stealing his designs. We figured it out, but just a little too late."

"What?" Beau stared at Nancy. "You mean Angel—"

"Was selling your designs to Budget Fashions," Nancy said, explaining how Bess had tricked the saleswoman in the Budget showroom. She also told them about the phone call she'd heard Angel make. "They were going to meet here at ten-thirty. When we arrived at quarter to eleven, Angel was dead. There was no sign of the killer."

"Poor Angel," Beau said, rubbing his eyes wearily. "It was lousy of him to steal my designs, but he didn't deserve to die."

The detective jotted notes on a clipboard. "Now, let me get this straight," he said to Nancy. "You think Angel was working with a partner, who turned on him tonight, stabbing him in the back?"

Nancy nodded.

"Any idea who this accomplice might be?" Detective Noonan persisted.

"There's Mrs. Chong," Nancy said speculatively. "After all, Angel was stabbed with her scissors."

"And she left the studio early today, without any explanation," Bess added.

"Mrs. Chong is *not* the killer," Beau said

wearily. "I've just spent the past five hours with her in the waiting room of Midtown Hospital."

Seeing the girls' surprised reactions, Beau explained. "Her husband was in surgery all night. I didn't finish up at the Plaza till six, so I went straight over to the hospital to stay with her. He's going to pull through just fine. But by the time I called in and got your message to meet you here, it was already well after ten."

"Did you find out how Mrs. Chong got the money for the operation?" Nancy asked him.

Beau nodded. "From her great-uncle."

"Why was the surgery such a secret?" Bess asked. "Angel wouldn't tell us anything about it."

"Mrs. Chong is very secretive about her personal life," Beau answered. "But Angel knew about the operation. In fact, he'd agreed to cover for us at the studio tonight."

"That makes sense," Nancy said, snapping her fingers. *"That's"* why Angel told the person on the phone to meet him here. He knew the studio would be empty, since you and Mrs. Chong would be at the hospital. And if one or two of the assistants had wanted to work late, he had the authority to send them home."

Detective Noonan pointed his pen at Nancy. "I like the way you work," he said.

"She's a great detective," Bess said. "Nancy's solved lots of famous cases."

"If Mrs. Chong is not the killer, we should check out Mimi Piazza," Nancy said thoughtfully. "I think that blue handkerchief sitting beside Angel's body might belong to her."

"That's quite a charge," the detective said. "Who is this Mimi?"

"Mimi Piazza, a rival designer," Beau said, explaining his history with the woman.

"Wait a minute," Nancy said, her mind racing. "When Angel was talking on the phone, he complained that he was taking all the risks, that the other person was *safe in a castle*. Mimi is known for being a security freak. And she would have a lot to lose if Angel revealed their theft to Delia Rogers, as he threatened on the phone."

"Sounds as if it might be worth checking this woman out," Detective Noonan agreed.

"In the meantime, are you going to search Angel's apartment for clues?" Nancy asked him.

"That's standard in a case like this." The detective nodded, then hesitated. "Why?"

"I'd like to go along," Nancy said. "There's a chance that Angel stole Joanna Rockwell's wedding gown. If he did, it might be stashed at his apartment."

"That's right," Bess said, perking up.

"The Rockwell heiress's gown," Noonan said, scratching his chin. "That wedding is the only thing my wife talks about these days. And you think the gown might be at Ortiz's apartment?"

"There's a chance," Nancy said hopefully.

"Angel rented a place in the East Village," Beau said. "I can show you where it is."

The detective lowered his clipboard and sighed. "Something tells me you people can't wait till tomorrow to check the place out."

"The gown contains pearls that are family heirlooms," Bess pointed out. "By tomorrow it might be gone."

Detective Noonan shrugged. "Let's go."

The detective pulled the unmarked police car to a stop in front of the old brownstone where Angel Ortiz lived. After Noonan opened a rear door for Nancy and Bess—there were no handles on the inside—they were able to climb out. They followed the two men through a waist-high wrought-iron gate and down a few steps to the door of the basement apartment.

"This is it," Beau said, "but we need to go upstairs and ask the landlord to let us in."

"Looks as if someone has already beat us here," Detective Noonan said.

Nancy peered over his shoulder and saw that the door was already ajar. The detective shoved it with the toe of his shoe until it was open. He stepped inside, and Nancy followed.

At first the only thing she could make out was darkness and clutter. Papers, cushions, and clothes were strewn everywhere.

"Either this guy was a slob or someone has searched this place," Detective Noonan muttered.

"Angel was impeccably neat," Beau said. "Someone must have been here."

Just then Nancy heard a noise coming from the rear of the apartment. Everyone froze.

"Get back," the detective said, motioning them toward the door.

As Nancy took a step back, she saw Detective Noonan reach inside his jacket and draw his revolver. He crept forward, stepped around a pile of clothes, then turned into a doorway.

Her heart beating like a drum, Nancy waited for a moment. She decided she couldn't stand back while Noonan might need help.

She tiptoed forward and found herself beside Detective Noonan in the doorway of a bathroom.

The same noise came again, and Nancy saw a flicker of movement in the opaque shower curtain drawn across the tub. Motioning for Nancy to wait, the detective raised his gun and inched forward.

Nancy held her breath as he ripped the curtain open.

A bare tub gleamed in the dim light. Nancy's eyes followed the tile up to a small open window, where a pair of feet were scurrying out!

Chapter
Thirteen

NANCY PUSHED past Noonan and jumped into the tub to grab one of the lace-up combat-style boots. Struggling to hold on, she saw that the intruder was a small, wiry guy, dressed in black jeans and a dark flak jacket. A black wool cap covered his head.

Beside her, the detective had clasped a hand over one of the man's legs. Nancy was about to pull him back into the tub when the intruder kicked wildly, knocking both Nancy and Noonan off balance.

"Yee—ow!" Nancy cried, slipping back against the tiled wall.

Detective Noonan shoved his pistol back into the holster and pulled himself up to the window. "There he goes," he said disgustedly.

Considering the small size of the window and

the lead the man had, Nancy doubted that they'd be able to catch him. "I'm going around front to see if I can snag him," the detective said, darting out the doorway.

Standing on tiptoes, Nancy checked out through the window. The bottom of the frame rested on the pavement of a small yard. She saw a clump of hedges on the left and a row of plastic trash cans on the right. Otherwise the dark yard was empty.

Nancy returned to the living room, where Bess and Beau had stood back while the detective raced out the front door. "There was a man hiding in the bathtub," Nancy explained. "He's probably the one who ransacked the place." She went to the door to check on the detective. Stepping outside, she spotted him coming down the stairs—alone.

"He got away," he said, marching back into the apartment. "But I got a sense of his size. He's thin as a twig and shorter than you," he said, nodding at Nancy.

"What about his hair?" Bess asked.

"Couldn't see it," Noonan said. "He was wearing a black wool cap."

"Did he have Joanna's gown?" Beau asked.

"Not unless he could have fit it in his pockets. He wasn't carrying anything."

Checking around the disheveled apartment, Nancy frowned. After seeing the handkerchief, she'd been sure Mimi was Angel's killer. Now they were looking for a thin, wiry man.

While Detective Noonan called to check in with the forensic team at Beau's studio, Nancy, Bess, and Beau searched Angel's apartment.

"Here's one of his sketchpads," Beau said, lifting the cardboard cover. The pages were blank, but from the indentations on the top sheet Nancy could tell that the pad had been used.

"Maybe Angel's partner came here for the last of the sketches," Nancy suggested.

"If that's the case, he missed these," Bess said, sliding rolled-up sketches out of a cardboard tube. "I found this under the sofa."

Beau and Nancy sifted through the sketches, which all bore the signature of Angel Ortiz in the bottom corner. "Some of these were Angel's designs," Beau said. "But three are mine, from the spring collection. He must have made duplicate sketches, then penciled in his signature."

"I wonder why?" Bess asked.

"He was anxious to get ahead, to make his mark as a designer," Beau said sadly. "I just didn't realize he was so ambitious."

"And what was in it for his partner?" Nancy asked aloud, wondering about the man who had squeezed out through the small window.

Detective Noonan hung up the phone and frowned. "The scissors were clean," he said. "We couldn't lift any fingerprints from them. But there was blood on the handkerchief. The lab will check it out."

"Sounds gruesome," Bess said, shivering.

By the time they finished searching Angel's apartment, it was well after midnight. Exhausted, Beau took a cab home. When Detective Noonan dropped the girls off at Eloise Drew's apartment, he told Nancy to keep him updated on her progress.

"I still think that handkerchief belongs to Mimi Piazza," Nancy said as she and Bess got ready for bed. "And that would place her at the scene of the murder. But I can't figure out who the intruder was at Angel's apartment."

"Maybe it was just a burglar," Bess said.

Nancy shook her head. "On the night of Angel's murder? Too coincidental. Maybe it was a thug hired by Michael Rockwell. Or maybe someone else was working with Angel and Mimi. . . ." She sank onto the bed as her thoughts wandered.

"What about Mimi's fashion show?" Bess asked, yawning. "Do you still want to go?"

"Definitely." Nancy nodded. "I've got to find out if Mimi Piazza was involved with Angel."

"Good morning, Ms. Rockwell." The guard in the black tuxedo smiled as he checked the guest list. "I have you down with two guests, a Ms. Drew and a Ms. Marvin."

"That's correct," Joanna said, glancing at Nancy and Bess. All three were elbow to elbow with the reporters waiting outside the showroom of Mimi Piazza's studio.

"Enjoy," the guard said, removing a velvet rope so the girls could squeeze by.

Inside the showroom, photographers jockeyed for position at the edge of the runway, a long platform stretching into the audience. The atmosphere was tense. Conversation buzzed through the room, and the seats were quickly filling up with spectators.

"Who are all these people?" Nancy asked.

"A lot of them are buyers from stores around the world," Bess explained. "Later on they'll meet with Mimi's people to discuss colors, delivery dates, and prices."

"Some are fashion editors from magazines and newspapers," Joanna said, waving at a woman across the room. "They'll critique Mimi's spring collection in their columns."

"Check out the runway," Bess said.

Painted black with a white line running down the center, the runway resembled a landing strip, complete with little red flashing lights at the edges. The backdrop was a brilliant blue sky dotted with wispy white clouds.

Just as the girls found three seats near the backstage door, Nancy heard Delia Rogers call out through the crowd.

"Joanna!" The silver-haired reporter rushed

over, camera crew in tow. "Is there any truth to the rumor that you're here to look for a new wedding gown?" she asked, pushing the microphone toward Joanna.

"Beau Winston is designing my bridal gown," Joanna stated, smiling at the camera. "But I do enjoy attending other designers' shows."

"Any news on your mother's pearls?" Delia probed. Before Joanna could answer, the music rose and stragglers rushed to their seats.

"They're starting!" Bess said excitedly.

Delia's crew pushed closer to the runway for a shot of the show's opening. The soaring noise of a landing jet came over the sound system as spotlights hit the runway and a chic-looking model strode out. She was wearing a skin-tight black gown with gold lamé sleeves that flared out behind her shoulders like wings.

"I guess the theme of the show is flying," Joanna said as a second model appeared, her arms raised to reveal a colorful pattern like that of a butterfly's wings on her sleeves.

Although the first few dresses were evening gowns, none of them resembled any of Beau's. "If Mimi was Angel's partner, she was smart enough not to use any of the stolen designs in her own collection," Nancy whispered to Bess, whose attention was riveted on the runway.

Everyone was mesmerized by the show. If Nancy was going to slip away and check out Mimi's studio, now was the time.

"I'll be back," she whispered to Bess, weaving through the crowd to reach the edge of the backdrop. She cut around behind it, went down a short hall and found herself backstage, in the middle of the feverish scramble.

Models in various stages of undress squeezed into gowns and tugged curlers out of their hair. Nancy paused behind an older woman, who was sewing a blond model into a red satin sheath.

"What made you think you could eat before a show?" the woman demanded. "Better suck it in when you get out there. Now go!" The woman cut the thread, pushed the model away, then turned to Nancy. "You're late! It's a good thing you're only modeling sportswear today."

Nancy blinked, then suddenly realized that the woman thought she was a model.

"Hey, Gloria," the woman called to someone a few racks away. "The redhead is here."

"Send her back!" came the answer.

"Chop, chop!" the older woman told Nancy. "You need to change—pronto!"

"Right away," Nancy told the woman. She maneuvered past models, scattered garment racks and stray shoes until she found a door that led away from the fray. The last thing she needed was to run into Gloria. She'd have to admit that she wasn't a model—or else take her chances on the runway!

Nancy found herself in a wide corridor cluttered with racks of clothes. Quickly she slid each garment down the rack, searching for Joanna's gown.

While she was checking, a uniformed guard walked by and gave her a curious look.

"Where is that dress?" she muttered aloud. "Gloria's going to kill me if I don't find it."

That seemed to satisfy the guard, who continued on, whistling softly.

Within minutes Nancy had checked every garment, but Joanna's gown wasn't there. Mimi would probably have locked it in a vault if she hadn't destroyed it, Nancy thought. She'd be better off searching Mimi's office for evidence that might tie the woman to Angel.

Nancy was about to head upstairs to the offices when the door behind her opened and the older woman stormed out.

"There you are! What are you doing out here?" she demanded, grabbing Nancy by the arm.

Nancy was about to answer when the door flew open again and a delicate woman with wispy red hair and dressed in an ivory suit with a lace hankie in the pocket came out. It was Mimi Piazza. "The redhead model is on the runway. I don't know what you're—" Mimi paused when she saw Nancy's face. "I know who *you* are," she rasped. "I saw you on 'Fashion Flash.' You're the detective who's working with Beau Winston."

"That's right," Nancy said.

"A spy." Mimi scowled, then told the older woman, "Get rid of her!"

Chapter

Fourteen

My name is Nancy Drew," Nancy said, breaking free of the other woman's hold. "I'm here with Joanna Rockwell."

"Is that true?" Mimi asked the older woman.

"I—I don't know," the flustered woman said. "I thought she was a model."

"You *thought?*" Mimi scoffed. "Go get security while I have a few words with Ms. Drew."

As the woman hurried off, Mimi sized up Nancy. "You have a lot of nerve sneaking around here," she said.

"Not as much nerve as it took for you to stab Angel Ortiz in the back with a pair of scissors."

Mimi's mouth dropped open in shock. "What a dreadful thing to say. Surely you don't believe I'd do anything like that." She spread her thin arms wide. "Look at me. I'm a ninety-eight-pound pushover, barely able to defend myself, much less murder anyone. That's why security is so important to me. Tell me, what were you looking for here?"

"Joanna Rockwell's gown," Nancy answered.

"And you think it's *here?*" Mimi rolled her eyes. "Sounds like another one of Beau's publicity stunts. I try to stay out of his business." She pushed a curl off her forehead, adding, "I just wish he'd stay out of mine."

Mimi's sweet smile made Nancy wonder if Beau had mistaken the woman's motives. She decided to take a chance and push a little harder.

"You know, Beau is convinced that you're responsible for Angel's death," Nancy said. "He says he has evidence incriminating you," she baited Mimi. "It's locked in his office."

"Evidence of what?" Mimi asked.

"Apparently, Angel taped every phone conversation he had with you," Nancy lied. She just hoped Mimi would believe her. "It's only a matter of time before the police—"

"I spoke with the police early this morning," Mimi interrupted her. "By the time we finished talking they apologized for disturbing me. You see, I haven't done anything wrong."

Just then two security guards burst into the hallway, cutting their conversation short.

"Escort Miss Drew back to the audience,"

Mimi told them. "And make sure she stays there."

After the show the girls joined Joanna for lunch at Rumpelmayer's, an old-fashioned soda shop across from Central Park that served triple-decker sandwiches and spectacular ice cream sundaes. As they ate, Nancy told Joanna and Bess about her encounter with Mimi.

"She sounds harmless," said Bess. "Do you really think she killed Angel?"

"I don't know," Nancy said, shaking her head. "It's possible that she was his partner, but she has a hard face to read. I wonder if the police have been able to identify the handkerchief yet."

"I can't believe you're investigating a murder," Joanna said, spooning a walnut from her sundae. "Now that Angel's gone, the theft of my gown is minor in comparison."

Nancy nodded. Angel's death had put a lot of things in perspective.

The workers at Beau Bridal were somber when Nancy and Bess arrived after lunch. The girls went into Beau's office to tell him what had happened at Mimi's show. Then Bess went off for a fitting, while Nancy went out to the workroom.

In the sunny workroom, Mrs. Chong was supervising final fittings for Beau's show.

"You're finished," she said, tapping Isis on the shoulder. "But don't you dare be late next week!"

As Nancy watched Mrs. Chong turn to a worktable to cut out a pattern piece, she realized how much the old woman had grown on her. Her brusque manner was just her way of getting things done.

"Terrible week," Mrs. Chong said. She stopped cutting and examined the scissors in her hand. "Angel is gone. And the killer took my best scissors."

"You'll get the scissors back," Nancy pointed out. "The police will return them after the trial." If there is a trial, she thought. So far, the police didn't even have a suspect.

"Not those scissors," Mrs. Chong said. "The ones the killer stole."

"Wait a minute." Nancy went over to the table and looked down at the open box of scissors. "There are *two* pairs of scissors missing?"

Mrs. Chong nodded. "Killer must have stolen one."

Nancy wondered why the killer would have made off with a pair of scissors. A thief would have taken the entire box. "Did you tell the police about the missing scissors?" she asked.

"I didn't waste their time," Mrs. Chong said, scowling. "Let them find Angel's killer instead."

"But the police should know about them," Nancy said, heading for the phone in Beau's office.

Detective Noonan listened while Nancy told

him about the missing scissors. "It appears that the killer took them," she told him. "Can you search Mimi's studio or home?"

"Not without a solid link between Mimi and the crime," he said.

"What about the handkerchief?" she asked.

"The blood on the handkerchief was Angel's," Noonan said. "It was the only bodily fluid on the cloth. We can't connect the handkerchief to Mimi. The intruder at Ortiz's apartment was a man. And when I interviewed Ms. Piazza, everything she said checked out. Frankly, I don't think Mimi Piazza is a killer."

As soon as the detective said goodbye, Nancy placed a call to her father in River Heights.

"I was going to call you at Eloise's apartment this evening," said Carson Drew. "I've been talking to people about Michael Rockwell. It appears his reputation is spotless, though his son had a scuffle with the law a few years back."

"Tyler?" Nancy said. "What happened?"

"He was charged with breaking and entering when he was a teenager. The charges were eventually dropped, but it seems the incident created a breach between father and son."

Nancy considered the information long after she'd said goodbye and hung up the phone. The feud between the Rockwell men was still going on. And it seemed that Joanna was stuck between them.

"What's happening?" Beau asked, entering the office with two bolts of cloth in his arms.

After updating him on the case, Nancy mentioned her suspicions about the Rockwell men. "It may sound crazy, but one of the Rockwells may have something to do with the disappearance of Joanna's gown. They're feuding, and Joanna's wedding seems to be the battleground."

"I had no idea that things were so bad with Joanna's family," Beau said. "But I can't imagine Michael Rockwell working with Angel."

"I can't, either," Nancy agreed.

"What about the intruder at Angel's apartment?" Beau asked hopefully.

Nancy considered the physique of the Rockwell men, then shook her head. "Joanna's father and brother are much taller than the guy in Angel's apartment."

That night, as Nancy watched Tyler perform on stage at the Players Theater, she felt a twinge of sympathy for Joanna's brother. Here he was, opening in his first off-Broadway show, and his father had chosen not to attend. Ironically, the show was about a family that had split up.

"My father is dead." Tyler spoke his lines somberly, but with a great deal of conviction. "He died the day he walked out that door."

Tears glimmered in the actor's eyes, and Nancy was moved by his performance.

After the show, Nancy, Bess, Joanna, and Sam huddled in the small actors dressing room backstage to congratulate Tyler.

Nancy recognized the other actors who drifted in and out. Some carried bouquets, others were chatting with friends.

"I'm sorry Dad couldn't make it," Joanna said as she gave her brother a hug. "You were great!"

"Thanks," Tyler said. "I'm glad you could make it, with all the wedding hoopla going on."

"Are you kidding?" Joanna said. "I wouldn't miss this for the world."

"It's a very moving show," Bess said. "I haven't cried so much for ages."

"Your father should see it," Sam said thoughtfully. "I think it would hit home."

"There's little chance of that." Tyler frowned. "He's too busy playing billionaire—when he's not telling you how to plan your wedding."

"Right now Dad's bossiness is the last thing on my mind," Joanna said sadly. "My gown is still missing—the one with Mom's pearls."

"Why are you taking it so hard?" Tyler asked.

Joanna's green eyes sparkled with tears. "For some reason, I feel as if I've let Mom down. And I'm worried about you. You should be in the wedding, Tyler. Mom would have wanted it."

Tyler bristled, clearly uncomfortable with his sister's suggestion.

"Don't pressure the guy on the night of his big

THE NANCY DREW FILES

debut," Sam said. "Now—take off your makeup and come celebrate with us."

"Great idea," Joanna agreed. "I'll get your coat. Where's your locker?"

Tyler paused, then gestured vaguely behind him. "It's over there." Nancy turned and noticed the name Rockwell written on tape on a battered locker door. Apparently, Tyler hadn't bothered to bring a padlock for it. Clear plastic wrap stuck out from the bottom, as if the locker was overloaded.

Before she or Joanna could go to it, Tyler ran his hand through his hair and said, "Look, I'm tired. I'd better take a raincheck."

Joanna protested, but Tyler was adamant. Finally she gave up, kissed her brother on the cheek, and said, "I'm so proud of you."

"Thanks, Sis," Tyler said quietly.

After a night of restless sleep, Nancy awoke early Friday morning. Bess slept quietly in the twin bed across the room. Tucking the soft comforter under her chin, Nancy stared at the ceiling and thought about the Rockwell family. She knew she had to be missing something important.

She knew that Michael Rockwell had been feuding with his son for years—probably since the time that Tyler was arrested for breaking and entering.

Just then she remembered crawling through the dark airshaft. The gown *could* have been stolen by an outsider.

Her mind flashed to Tyler, last night in the dressing room. She remembered Tyler's locker. It was the one with plastic wrap sticking out. It was just like the plastic that covered dresses that were wheeled through the garment district.

"Oh, no!" She sat up in bed.

"What's wrong?" Bess asked, rubbing her eyes.

"Get dressed," Nancy said as she threw back the covers. "We're about to solve another piece of the puzzle."

"Give me three minutes," Bess muttered.

By the time the girls arrived at the Players Theater, it was barely nine o'clock.

"The place looks dead," Bess said, peering into the dark box office.

"Let's try the stage door," Nancy said.

They pounded hard on the side door, then waited. Finally, it swung open. "What is it?" asked a gray-haired man. From his uniform, Nancy guessed that he was a custodian.

"We left something in the men's dressing room," Nancy told him. "And we need it right away. It's urgent."

The man rolled his eyes, then held the door open for them. "Come on," he said. "I haven't got all day." The janitor followed the girls to the room.

Nancy's pulse raced as she darted toward the locker marked Rockwell. She gave the handle a tug, and the door swung open. Inside, she found an ocean of white under clear plastic wrap.

She reached in and pulled out a white dress with hundreds of glimmering antique seed pearls. "It's Joanna's gown!"

Chapter

Fifteen

Y OU FOUND IT!" Bess cried, patting Nancy on the shoulder. "You figured it all out!"

The custodian scratched his head, confused. "Is that a costume?" he asked.

"More or less," came a voice from the doorway. Nancy turned to see Tyler. He stepped into the room, tugging his sister behind him.

"What's the big surprise?" Joanna stumbled to a halt when she saw Nancy and Bess. "Did Tyler drag you guys here, too?" she asked, then gasped when her eyes lit on the gown in Nancy's arms.

"My gown!" Joanna let out a whoop of joy as she rushed across the room to take the gown. Sliding one hand under the plastic, she touched the shimmering seed pearls and counted the larger ones along the neckline.

"Mom's pearls are here, safe and sound, and

the gown looks lovely," Joanna said, astounded. "But how did it get here?"

"I brought it here," Tyler confessed. "Nancy must have figured out the truth, which is—well, I owe you all an apology. I took the gown from Beau's studio."

"You did?" Confused, Joanna frowned.

Tyler's face turned red as he nodded. "I got through the lobby door of Beau's building with a credit card. The studio door was unlocked, and the place was quiet, though I knew someone was working in that little room in the corner."

That would have been Mrs. Chong, Nancy realized as she listened to his explanation.

"I knew the vault was impossible to open," Tyler continued, "so I sneaked into the workroom and climbed through the air shaft."

"But how did you know it led to the vault?" Nancy asked.

"I'd been in Beau's studio before," Tyler explained. "I came with Joanna once for a fitting. I noticed that vent in the vault. It struck me that the airshaft would be an easy way for a crook to get into the vault."

"Why did you do it?" Joanna asked him. There was a catch in her voice and anguish in her eyes.

"When Dad insisted on running your wedding, I couldn't stand it," Tyler admitted. "I wanted to see the look on his face when the gown of the century turned up missing."

"But your plan backfired," Nancy said.

Tyler nodded. "After Sam dragged me into the wedding rehearsal, and after you guys came to my show last night . . ." He stared down at the floor, ashamed. "I realized that I'd messed up, big time." He turned to his sister. "I was hurting you—the one person who really cares about me."

Touching the gown, he added, "Besides, Mom would want you to wear her pearls on the most important day of your life."

Joanna bit her lip, as if holding back her anger. "It was a lousy thing to do, Tyler," she told her brother. "I don't know how you could pull such a stunt—even to get back at Dad." Joanna paused then, as if collecting herself. "Right now I just want to get this dress to a safe place."

"But there's still the matter of catching Angel's murderer," Nancy said, turning to Joanna. "And with your help, I'd like to lay a trap to snag the killer—whoever it is!"

Together, Nancy, Bess, Joanna, and Tyler took the bridal gown and piled into the Rockwell limousine, which was waiting outside the theater. Following Nancy's plan, they went straight to the Rockwell apartment, where they were met by the usual army of doormen and guards.

"You were right about this building," Bess said as they streamed through the lobby, following a guard to the Rockwells' private elevator. "It's got to be one of the safest places in New York."

Nancy nodded as the elevator doors whooshed shut. "That's why Joanna's gown is going to stay here until tomorrow's wedding—though we'll need to make everyone think that the gown is sitting in Beau's studio."

Inside the spacious apartment, Joanna asked the cook to prepare brunch for everyone, while Nancy sat down beside the phone in the library and called Beau's studio.

"We found Joanna's gown!" Nancy told him. "And Joanna's willing to help us catch Angel's killer."

Beau was thrilled to hear about the gown, though he said he never would have guessed that Tyler had taken it. By the time Nancy and Beau concocted a plan, the Rockwell cook had laid out trays of food on the dining room table. There were platters of eggs and Canadian bacon, bowls of fruit, and baskets of warm muffins and danishes.

"I just spoke to Sam," Joanna said as she served herself a healthy portion of eggs. "He's ecstatic about the gown. He said to thank you a million times, Nancy. You've been a big help."

"Beau is sending Mrs. Chong over to take care of any last-minute alterations on the gown," Nancy told everyone as she buttered a steaming cranberry muffin. "He's also one hundred percent behind the plan."

"What are you going to use as bait?" Tyler asked.

"Beau is going to wrap up the bridal gown they have at the studio—Joanna's second choice," Nancy explained. "We'll put it in his office, so it's not too difficult to get to."

"That's the part I don't understand," Joanna said as she passed the eggs to Bess. "Why would the killer bother? Why would anyone return to Beau's studio just to steal my gown?"

"If Mimi is the accomplice, she might come back. I twisted the truth when I met her yesterday at the fashion show," Nancy said. "Mimi thinks Angel taped their phone conversations. I told her that Beau has the tapes locked up in his office."

Tyler's eyes widened. "That's some motivation. If Mimi was Angel's partner, she'll have to go after those tapes eventually. I'm surprised she didn't try last night."

"With her show yesterday it would have been too hectic. I'm sure she was partying and busy late into the night," Nancy explained.

"With the wedding gown right there, I doubt if Mimi could resist taking it," Bess added.

"Bess and I will be watching from the storage room next to Beau's office. If Mimi's not the guilty party, maybe we'll snag the guy who searched Angel's apartment."

"I know word travels fast in the fashion world," Tyler said, "but how can you be sure Angel's partner will hear about Joanna's gown in time?"

"The power of the press," Nancy said, smiling.

"Joanna's going to call Delia Rogers as soon as we finish eating. We'll hold a press conference at Beau's studio today at three o'clock. A story this hot should merit a special feature on 'Fashion Flash.'"

The day flew by as Nancy and Bess arranged the press conference at Beau's studio. With reporters wanting statements and last-minute wedding questions for the bride, the phone at the apartment rang constantly.

Nancy and Bess also got to meet the two bridesmaids they had stood in for. While Joanna was sequestered with Mrs. Chong, Nancy and Bess coached the girls on the details of the next day's ceremony.

By the time three o'clock rolled around they were ready and waiting at Beau Bridal. The reception area of the studio was crowded with reporters. Nancy and Bess stood in the doorway of the workroom, watching with interest.

Delia Rogers was at the center of the swarming pack, tossing off questions in her rapid-fire manner. "When did you find the gown?" she asked. "Where was it? Is it damaged?"

"The gown is in perfect shape," Joanna said. "I've been told that it was accidentally shipped out to the wrong party. It's a miracle that Beau managed to find it in time for my wedding."

"Can we see the dress?" a reporter asked.

"Before the wedding?" Joanna raised her eyebrows. "This bride's had enough bad luck."

"The gown is safe in my office," Beau said, "where it will stay until the wedding tomorrow morning. We're doing some final alterations, but I've promised Joanna that they'll be complete by the time my staff and I leave the studio tonight."

"Are you sure you're going to be okay?" Beau asked as he peered into the storeroom. Nancy, Bess, and Joanna were holed up against one wall with flashlights, comfortable quilts, and a stack of fashion magazines. It was already after nine, and Beau was getting ready to leave for the day. "Maybe I should stay. I hate to leave you girls alone."

"But you have to go," Nancy pointed out. "Angel's partner won't make a move until he or she sees you leave the building."

"We'll be fine," Bess assured him. "I've been on stakeouts with Nancy before. Believe me, the worst part is the waiting. It's a bore!"

"Are you sure?" Beau asked. "Maybe—"

"Good night, Beau," Joanna said firmly.

After Beau left, Nancy turned out the overhead light and stretched out on a quilt. Joanna and Bess had their heads together over a bridal magazine lit by one of the flashlights. "I'm amazed you're here with us, Joanna," Nancy said. "Your wedding is just hours away."

Joanna laughed. "It's my last night out with the girls, and I'm going to make the most of it! Besides, if you guys can stay up all night and still make it to my wedding, I can, too."

"Unfortunately, Bess was right about stake-outs being boring," Nancy admitted. "I just hope this one pans out."

The girls settled in for a long wait. Only twenty minutes later, Nancy thought she heard the sound of a door opening.

"Someone's here," she said, shushing the others. Kneeling against the wall to Beau's office, Nancy put her eye up to the peephole and waited.

Within minutes the light flicked on and a slight man entered. Dressed in black from his combat boots to his wool cap, the man moved quietly about the office, digging through file drawers. As the man turned, Nancy got her first glimpse of his face, but his features were distorted by a nylon stocking worn over his head.

"It's the guy we saw in Angel's apartment," Nancy whispered as she turned to her friends.

Peering into the office again, she saw the man wheel toward the gown. He pulled a shiny object out of his jacket pocket. Nancy gasped as the light glimmered on the golden handles of Mrs. Chong's scissors!

Fiendishly, he cut the bridal gown into shreds. Then he shoved the scissors back into the pocket of his jacket.

"Get this," Nancy whispered to the girls. "He didn't steal the gown—he *shredded* it."

"Can you see his face?" Bess asked. "Can I look?"

"It's distorted by a stocking." Nancy slid away from the crack to give Bess a chance.

Bess settled herself close to the wall, then began craning her neck around to get a better view. "But, Nancy," Bess said after a minute, "I don't see anyone there at all."

Nancy scrambled back to the crack in the wall. There was no one there! The intruder had gone.

All of a sudden she sniffed something odd. Smoke! She turned her head, trying to see the rest of the office. Then her eyes jumped to a pile of papers on Beau's desk. They lit up in a yellow-orange glow, then crackled and exploded in flame.

"He's set the place on fire!" Nancy gasped.

"It's the only way he can be sure that all the evidence against him is destroyed," Bess said.

"I smell smoke now, too!" Joanna exclaimed.

Nancy rushed to the door. It was hot, which meant the fire was close. The intruder must have started another blaze in the hallway.

"Stay down and move over there," Nancy said, pointing to the opposite wall. The girls dropped into a crouching position and scrambled across the storeroom.

Nancy touched the door handle, then yanked

her hand away. "We'll never get out this way," she said, crawling over to where Bess and Joanna were crouched against the wall. The beams of their flashlights illuminated the doorway, where wisps of black smoke were beginning to leak around the frame.

"What are we going to do?" Joanna asked.

Just then the smoke was followed by the first lick of flame that wrapped around the bottom of the wooden door. The fire is here, Nancy thought as she sank back between two plywood studs. And we're trapped!

Chapter

Sixteen

"THERE HAS to be another way out of here," Joanna said, moving the beam of her flashlight around the room.

"And we'd better find it! That smoke is choking me," Bess said.

"Cover your mouth with this," Joanna suggested, handing Bess a swatch of cloth.

In the distance Nancy could hear smoke alarms begin to ring, but she knew by the time the fire department arrived, they'd be dead from smoke inhalation.

"We have to get out!" Bess exclaimed.

Using the beam of her flashlight, Nancy searched the room. She had to stay calm. Recalling what she knew about Beau's studio, she remembered the ventilation system. "There's got to be a vent in here!"

Thinking through the floor plan, Nancy turned to the wall behind her. She had to push through a rack of clothes, but at last she found the square opening. "The vent!" she shouted. Using her penknife as a lever, she pried off the vent cover and let it drop to the floor.

Just then Nancy heard the noise of wood popping in the heat. Looking back, she saw that the door was now enveloped in flames.

It was now or never.

"Quick! Crawl out this way!" Nancy shouted. She gave Bess a boost into the air shaft.

Joanna was next, then Nancy tried to follow, but couldn't reach the opening without a boost.

She searched the dark room for something to stand on, then dragged a broken dress form over and set it on its side to use as a step. At last, she was able to dive into the vent, her hips scraping the jagged edges of the opening as she slithered through.

The air shaft was like a dark tunnel, made all the more eerie by the bouncing beams of the girls' flashlights and the occasional squeak of their sneakers against the metal lining. Nancy forged ahead, following Bess and Joanna. When they reached a juncture, Bess stopped. Nancy thought hard about the layout of the studio, and took her best guess about which way to tell her to go.

A minute or so later Nancy reached the end of the shaft. Coughing and covered with dust, she popped her head into the workroom, where water was pouring from the sprinklers in the ceiling.

Joanna and Bess grabbed Nancy's arms and helped her to her feet.

"This way," Nancy shouted over the alarms. She led Bess and Joanna out through the reception area, then darted toward the stairs.

Outside, the night air was cool, but it was a welcome relief. Nancy doubled over, then straightened up and took a deep breath.

"You two sure know how to show a girl a good time," Joanna said, wiping dust and soot from her face.

Bess coughed. "A real hot time."

"We'd better call nine-one-one," Nancy said. "The fire department will probably respond to the alarms, but it can't hurt to make sure."

"I'll go," Bess said, pointing to a phone booth at the end of the street. Joanna followed.

Checking to her right, Nancy watched her friends disappear behind a newsstand. Then she moved to the building next door and sat down on the stone threshold. She was wondering if the fire fighters would be able to find Beau's studio when a dark figure stepped out of a nearby vestibule.

Taking in the black clothes and lace-up boots, Nancy knew it was Angel's killer. He must have stopped to see whether the fire caught. "Wait a minute," Nancy called.

The man darted down the block, then turned into a dark alley. Nancy was on his heels, lunging

141

forward and grabbing for his jacket, but caught his cap instead. The man tripped and fell, throwing Nancy off balance. She stumbled, still clutching the cap, which was yanked off his head. Nancy managed to get her bearings and back off as he spun around.

Shock rippled through Nancy as she looked into his face. *He* was a *woman!* It was Mimi Piazza in men's clothing. Now that the cap was gone, there was no mistaking the red ringlets.

"Stay out of my business!" Mimi hissed, getting to her feet.

"It's too late for that," Nancy answered. "I know that you killed Angel. And soon the police will have enough evidence to convict you."

The corner of Mimi's mouth lifted in a sneer. "Your precious evidence is burning away up there," she said, pointing toward Beau's studio.

Not all of it, Nancy thought, remembering that after shredding the wedding gown Mimi had tucked Mrs. Chong's scissors into her pocket. But she didn't want to reveal her hand to Mimi. Instead, she said, "Who masterminded the design theft? Was it you or Angel?"

"There's no way I can be tied to those stolen designs," Mimi said, her dark eyes glittering. "That's the glory of it. Angel came to me for a job, and instead I planted a little idea in his brain. I even introduced him to the buyers at Budget, to start the ball rolling."

Nancy nodded. "So Angel stole three of Beau's designs and sold them to Budget as his own. He took the risk, but you had the satisfaction of knowing you were undermining Beau, your rival since design school."

"You're a clever girl," Mimi said, peeling off the stocking that distorted her features. "But you still don't have a case against me."

"But things weren't happening fast enough for Angel," Nancy speculated. "He wanted recognition for his own designs. He thought Beau was holding him back, and he realized that you weren't doing him any favors, either."

"He had the nerve to give me an ultimatum," Mimi complained, reaching into her pocket and pulling out a pair of leather gloves. "If I didn't hire him and give him his own label at my design house, he was going to blackmail me, making it look as if *I* was the one stealing Beau's designs."

"Why didn't you give him a job as a designer?" Nancy asked, aware of the sirens and horns of approaching fire trucks. What was taking them so long?

"Have you seen his designs?" Mimi scoffed, slipping the gloves on. "Garbage. His ego was larger than his talent. I had no choice but to—get rid of him."

When Mimi reached into her pocket again, Nancy stepped back defensively. She remembered the contents of that pocket all too well.

A moment later her fears were realized as Mimi pulled the scissors out and lifted them in the air. The nightmarish vision of the woman lunging toward her sent Nancy stumbling backward.

As Mimi thrust the scissors forward, Nancy dodged her, backing into a trash can, then scrambling around it. Mimi was ready to strike again, but Nancy was a few steps ahead of her. She turned to run and barreled into the solid form of Detective Noonan.

"That's enough," the officer said, quickly sizing up the scene. He moved Nancy aside, drew his pistol, and pointed it at Mimi. "Police!" he shouted.

Stunned, Mimi blinked, her rage fading as she let Mrs. Chong's scissors fall to the sidewalk. "You don't understand, officer," she said. "This girl was robbing me. I was defending myself—"

"Right," Detective Noonan said. "And those wouldn't happen to be scissors from Mrs. Chong's collection?"

"I don't know what you're talking about!" Mimi insisted indignantly.

"We'll see about that," the detective said. He snapped a pair of handcuffs around Mimi's wrists and recited her rights to her.

Relief washed through Nancy like a warm wave. She turned toward the fire trucks that had begun pulling into the street. Bess and Joanna were standing behind them, wrapped in blankets. One fire fighter handed Nancy a wool blanket, then scurried off to assist on the ladder truck.

Nancy looked up at the smoke pouring out through the broken windows of the workroom.

At last it was over.

Thirty minutes later, the fire had been doused and the damage was being assessed. Beau had rushed to the scene as soon as he was called. Sam Hollingsworth had also shown up when Tyler told him how his fiancée was spending the evening.

"Are you nuts?" Sam told Joanna. "You could have been killed!"

He stood near the girls, who sat on the tailgate of one of the rescue vehicles.

"Just as crazy as you are every time you climb into a race car," Joanna pointed out.

Sam pulled her into his arms and held her close. "It's hard to accept that risk when it involves someone you love."

"I know," Joanna said. "But it's a fact of life."

Just then Beau came out of the building, followed by Detective Noonan and a fire chief.

"The fire took its toll," Beau reported, "but everything in the vault is safe. We can go on with next week's show as planned. But I'll have to look for new studio space."

"Thank goodness!" Bess said. "I'd just die if

something happened to those beautiful gowns for the Petite Elite line."

"I'm just glad that you girls are safe," Beau said, squeezing Nancy's arm.

"And we have a solid case against Mimi Piazza," Detective Noonan announced. "I just got word from the precinct. They found traces of blood inside the pocket of Mimi's jacket. The lab will run tests to see if it's Angel's blood, but it's almost a moot point now. Mimi has confessed to the murder of Angel Ortiz."

"Finally," Nancy said, sighing. "But why did she steal the second pair of scissors?"

"Mimi says she panicked after she stabbed Angel," Noonan said. "She was afraid she'd run into someone on her way out of the studio. She took the second pair of scissors just in case."

"I'm glad that's solved," Bess said, yawning. "Now we'd all better get some sleep," she told the group. "Tomorrow's a big day, and I want to be on my toes for the wedding!"

Surrounded by her camera crew, Delia Rogers was interviewing guests on the steps of St. Patrick's Cathedral when Nancy and Bess arrived the next day. Nancy caught a snippet of conversation as she walked past.

"As you can see," Delia said, "rock 'n' roll idol Izzy Green is decked out in a leather tux for the occasion. Tell us, Izzy, do you—"

"That was Izzy Green," Bess muttered as she followed Nancy into the front vestibule of the cathedral. "He looks skinnier in person."

"You have all day to check out the celebrities," Nancy reminded her friend. "But if we want to wish Joanna luck, we've got to hurry. The wedding starts in ten minutes."

As she walked through the cathedral, Nancy smoothed the bodice of her blue velvet gown. The purple satin skirt of Bess's dress rustled as she hurried alongside Nancy.

The girls found their way to a small room off the side of the altar. Bridesmaids dressed in emerald green gowns fluttered around Joanna, who was pinning her headpiece to her dark hair. Beau stood off to the side, double-checking the gowns worn by the bridal party.

"Nancy! Bess!" Joanna called. "Come on in and join the party." Even in the dimly lit room, Joanna seemed to sparkle.

"You look absolutely gorgeous!" Bess said.

"Thanks." Joanna smoothed her hands over the beaded bodice then reached out to tug Nancy and Bess closer. "Beau's dress really highlights Mom's pearls—and thanks to you two, I get to wear them!"

"Looks like everyone is set here," Beau said, kissing Joanna on the cheek. "I'll see you later."

"Save us a place in the cathedral!" Bess called after Beau as he left the room.

"You'll never believe what happened last night when I got home," Joanna said. "Fireworks!"

"What?" Nancy said, confused.

"Dad blew up when he heard that I was involved in the stakeout," Joanna explained. "There was a huge argument. Sam and Tyler got involved, too."

"What was the outcome?" Bess asked.

Joanna shrugged. "Everyone had a chance to air their feelings. Tyler and Dad seem to be willing to talk now. And Sam has reached a new understanding with my father. When my mother was alive, she was the glue that kept us together. Now I guess it's up to me. And I think I've made a good start."

"Your mother would be proud of you," Nancy said, squeezing Joanna's hand. In the distance she heard the thrum of organ music. "We'd better get outside," she told Bess. "Or else we'll make Joanna late for her own wedding!"

Out in the cavernous cathedral, Nancy and Bess were escorted to the pew where Beau was sitting. Soon the wedding march began, and a sweet feeling swept through Nancy as the music played. One by one, bridesmaids proceeded down the aisle, arm in arm with the handsome ushers.

Looking to her left, Nancy saw tears sparkling in Bess's blue eyes.

"It's so romantic," Bess said.

148

At last Joanna walked down the aisle with her father. The pearls in her dress held a warm glow that matched her smile. Nancy had never seen a more beautiful bride.

"This wedding is going to be the happiest ever," Bess said. "All thanks to you, Nan."

Nancy's next case:

Famed actress Evelyn Caldwell has put her career and her money on the line. Her ambition is to transform a Connecticut barn into a big-time theater. But the play she has in production may turn into a real barn-burner: Someone has threatened to bring the house down—in a single burst of flame!

That's when Nancy gets into the act. Together with Ned and George, she's come to the New England countryside to search behind the scenes for a saboteur. She also begins to suspect that a certain female cast member is out to sabotage something else: Nancy's own relationship with Ned. The plot is heating up—and Nancy's the one who stands to get burned . . . in *Stage Fright,* Case #90 in The Nancy Drew Files™.

THE HARDY BOYS® CASE FILES